LOVING LYNN CELIA

*A Novel of the French and Indian War on
the Southern Frontier*

G.G. Stokes, Jr.

Loving Lynn Celia

ISBN 9780615534374

Printed in the United States of America

G.G. Stokes, Jr.

Table of Contents

G.G. Stokes, Jr.

PROLOGUE

Simpson's Meadow, South Carolina
August 28, 1833

The old man sat in his rocker and sighed. Two of his small great-great-grandchildren scurried on hands and knees about the floor, exploring the nooks and crannies of the old log house while their mother, his great-granddaughter, lifted the lid from a pot of stew simmering over the open fire in the hearth. Perspiration beaded along her forehead and trickled from beneath the band of her mobcap to flow in thin rivulets down the side of one rosy cheek. Strangely, he felt cool.

He patted the back of his wife's hand. It lay atop the thin white sheet that covered her as she slumbered throughout the hot afternoon. She smiled without opening her eyes. He studied her face, amazed at the intricate network of crow's feet that had crept across it over the years and at the thinness of her snow-white hair. She would turn one-hundred years old tomorrow, and old Doc Hatcher had said if she lived to see it, it would be a miracle. Of course, this wasn't the Doc Hatcher of his younger days, but his grandson, now also wrinkled with age.

He reached up with his free hand and unconsciously rubbed his chest. The burning sensation that had kept him awake for the past week faded as a bittersweet feeling of sadness overwhelmed him. He looked at his wife again and thought of how quickly their lives had passed. He could remember seeing her for the first time. When was it? Forty years ago? Fifty? It seemed like yesterday. He chuckled aloud as he silently accused himself of senility. His granddaughter cut her eyes in his direction and gave him a small, indulgent smile.

He smiled back and settled into the rocker, closing his eyes as he calculated the years he had spent loving this woman. His thoughts drifted back to a beautiful morning on the Savannah River when their paths had first crossed. He nodded to himself, satisfied and amazed. It had been seventy-seven years ago that he had first laid eyes on the woman he was destined to spend his life with. He rubbed the tips of his fingers across his smallpox-ravaged face, thinking back to when he was young, so young—as was she.

* * * *

"Grandpaps," his granddaughter shook his arm to gain his attention. The movement startled him. He hadn't realized he had dozed off. His first thought was for his wife. He reached out and rested the palm of his hand lightly atop her chest, then sighed with relief when he felt it rise.

6

He looked back at his granddaughter. "Are you leavin', Eunice?"

Her name reminded him of her namesake, also once young and beautiful, already dead for twenty years. The memory brought tears to his eyes as the new Eunice patted him on the arm again.

"I'll see you first thing in the morning," she said in little more than a whisper. "There's stew warmin' by the fire, if'n you get hungry."

"No need to hurry over. I think we'll sleep late."

She kissed him on the forehead. "I'll see you tomorrow," the old man said again. But he knew he wouldn't. If his wife passed tonight, he had no wish to continue alone.

He waited until Eunice had gone before he pushed himself to his feet. It took all of his strength to rise. He rubbed his chest again. How it burned! And that cramp in his left shoulder just kept on naggin' at him. He rolled his arm to work out the stiffness in it and told himself he had best skip supper tonight.

Leaving a long taper burning in a glass-sided lantern; he shed his clothing and slid beneath the covers alongside his sleeping wife. He moved slowly, taking great care not to wake her.

Piling up two feather pillows, he rolled onto his side so he could watch her sleep. He had always enjoyed their moments alone. His thoughts glided back through all those long years. He remembered she had once been beautiful. He leaned forward and kissed her on the cheek.

As if reading his mind, she smiled in her sleep and mumbled, "I remember," in a voice so soft it almost escaped him.

It suddenly dawned on him that, to him, she was still the most beautiful woman in the world. His mind began to wander through all the lost years. He could see her now, as she had been in those days.

CHAPTER ONE

Thomas Simpson stretched his long, corded arms indolently over his head as he yawned and shook his body in the crisp morning air. He was not a tall man, little more than five feet nine, but years of guiding his father's flatboat through the submerged snags of the Savannah River had left him with a square physique. He seemed almost as wide as he was tall. His demeanor suggested unlimited endurance, his face conveyed unlimited kindness.

He stood on the deck of the flatboat, moored on the Georgia bank of the Savannah River. He yawned and stretched as he turned to look towards the shore where his father sat on a log, tending their breakfast over a smoky fire. The flatboat's crew lounged indolently around the small clearing, sitting up in their crumpled blankets, half-awake and waiting on their breakfast. They were two days out of Augusta, halfway through their downriver journey to Savannah. Their cargo—five tons of prime deerskins.

A slight mewing sound caught Thomas's attention and arrested his movement. He tilted his head to one side, focusing on the source of the sound. He heard it again; it was coming from beneath a tarp stretched between two bales of pressed buckskins. Shaking his head, he pulled the cover back, expecting to see a mother cat with a brood of kittens. His eyes widened in surprise as he looked down, instead, at a slovenly dressed woman nursing an infant. She looked up at him, her eyes bright blue, firm, and defiant.

"What do we have here? A stowaway?" He smiled as he spoke. "I thought that only happened on the tall ships down to Savannah." He studied her face as he talked, gauging the tone of his words; they were meant to put her at ease. He held out his hand, offering to help her rise. The woman made no attempt to take it. Her eyes darted towards the shore, then returned to him. Thomas dropped the tarp back over her and let his hand fall to his side.

"Suit yourself," he said, speaking to her through the tarp. "I'm goin' to get some breakfast. Come on over to the fire if'n you're hungry." With that, he headed for the cooking fire.

Taking a seat alongside his father, he leaned forward, resting his elbows on his thighs. He made no mention of the woman, sensing that at some point he may need to deny ever having seen her. She had that look about her. Probably a runaway indentured servant from South Carolina fleeing an abusive master, or husband. She would most likely be gone when he returned, fleeing in search of an uncertain future, pursuing the slight promise of a better life.

The men had just finished their breakfasts, and Thomas and his father were preparing to take their turns at scrubbing the frying pan and tin plates in the river, when the rumble of approaching horses drifted to them from the south. The unknown riders were moving rapidly in their direction. The men exchanged wary glances. Thomas's father jerked his head in the direction of the flatboat, his meaning was clear.

Thomas dropped the frying pan and hopped onto the squared timbers of the boat. Entering the small sleeping compartment located in the middle of the craft, he snatched a brass-barreled blunderbuss from its pegs on the wall. He flipped the frizzen open to check the priming and snapped it shut with a metallic click. Pulling the hammer to full cock, he stood to one side of the open door, out of view of anyone on the shore, waiting as the rumble grew louder. In the clearing, the other boatmen were fingering the knives and tomahawks stuffed into their belts. The man who had been assigned guard duty stepped behind the trunk of a large water oak, musket in hand, and waited.

Thomas's father continued to stand at the river's edge, facing the approaching horsemen; there were four of them. They reined in when they saw the group of rivermen. Two of them separated from the group and approached. One of them held up his hand in greeting.

"How goes it?" he asked. "I'm Sheriff Wright, from Savannah. We're looking for a young woman with a babe in arms." The sheriff spoke like a man in a great hurry. "To whom do I have the honor of speaking?" He directed the question towards Thomas's father.

"I am Richard Simpson, of Augusta. Heading down to Savannah with a load of skins."

"Pleased to meet you," the sheriff said. He jerked his head to indicate the other man sitting impatiently at his side. "The woman stole a broach and gold ring worth more'n twenty-five pounds from Mr. Savage here." He paused, waiting for an answer.

Richard shook his head, "No, sir. I haven't seen a woman since we left Augusta two days ago. What's she look like? Just in case I happen on her."

Before Sheriff Wright could answer, Thomas stepped from the flatboat's cabin. "Mornin'," he said with a slight nod of his head. He eased the hammer to half cock and set the blunderbuss out of sight, behind the door.

"Mornin'," the sheriff replied. "You seen a dark-haired woman with a sucklin' babe, son?"

Thomas pretended to think for a moment. "No sir, I ain't. What'd she do?"

"Thievery."

Thomas nodded, but said nothing. He leaned one shoulder against the doorframe and folded his arms. The sheriff looked around at the other faces in the clearing, gave his wide-brimmed hat a quick tug, said, "Thank you," spun his mount around, and continued his race northward. The other three riders followed at his heels.

"Now that's a job I couldn't have," Richard muttered.

"Sheriff!" one of the boatmen said in a disparaging tone. "How many men does it take to bring in one woman and her babe?"

Thomas spent the remainder of the day using his pole to steer the boat clear of submerged snags in the river. Twice he paused long enough to fill the water bucket from the river and, after offering a dipper full of the cool liquid to his father and the

13

other six crewmen, sat the bucket beside the tarp where he was certain the woman was still hiding. He never saw her, but when he looked a few moments later, the dipper was gone.

After Thomas finished his lunch, he left half of his cornbread beside the bales of skins, within easy reach of the woman's hiding place.

That evening, they tied the boat to a gnarled oak limb waving like a lonely sentinel over the river. They would spend their last night here before floating down to Savannah the following morning.

Thomas stayed on the boat to tighten the lashings on the cargo while the rest of the crew kindled a fire and began preparing a meager supper ashore. When it was ready, his father waved him over.

"Bring that stowaway with you," he said casually.

Caught off guard, Thomas hesitated. He turned and lifted the tarp. Looking down into those bright blue eyes, he smiled and said, "Come on out ma'am, it's suppertime."

The woman rose stiffly, the sleeping infant nestled against the nape of her neck. "Thank you, sir," she said with a tired smile. Thomas moved to one side, watching her as she made her way to the fire. She sat using her soiled skirt as a cushion.

14

They ate in silence. When they had finished, the woman looked around the small circle of men, studying their faces. Her gaze settled on Thomas and his father.

"Thank you," she said, "I was famished."

"Our pleasure," both men answered. Thomas reached for the woman's plate. She stopped him. "If you will allow me to lay Roger on one of the cots in the boat's cabin, I'll wash the dishes. It's the least I can do in payment for such a delicious meal."

Richard and Thomas, along with the other men, sat smoking their pipes and digesting their meals while they watched the woman work. She was a tiny thing, not quite five feet tall, probably no more than ninety pounds. Her hair was as black as a Raven's wing and would have been as shiny except for the series of tangles and rat nests in it. The woman sensed their eyes on her; she turned and smiled over her shoulder before returning to her work.

"You reckon she's the woman the sheriff was askin' after?" Thomas said. He looked towards his father.

The other men in the circle grinned; they had known that from the moment they had clapped eyes on her.

"Can't be no one else, I'd say," Richard answered. A wisp of gray tobacco smoke curled from his mouth as he spoke. "She don't look like a thief to me, though." He looked around at the faces of his crew. "Y'all keep this to yourselves," he said, punctuating his words with short stabs of his clay pipe. The tone of his words made it an unmistakable order.

"She don't look like one to me neither," Thomas agreed. He stood and left the fire. Stooping beside the woman, he gathered up the clean plates while she scoured the tin cups with river sand. "You're welcome to travel with us a spell," he told her.

She turned her head, studying his face. "That's kind of you, but you do realize *I am* the woman the sheriff's looking for, don't you?"

Thomas nodded. "He says you're a thief. You don't look like one."

The woman laughed at his apparent bashfulness. "Thank you!" she said and laughed again. "May I ask what a thief looks like?"

Thomas blushed, "Well, er … I don't rightly know ma'am. I've only seen a few, and they didn't look like you. You have a way about you." He paused, seeming to search for the right words, before continuing, "For one thing, you speak and carry yourself like a lady. You're fairly different from the womenfolk around here. May I ask where you're from?"

"Wiltshire, in England. I've only been in the colonies for a few weeks. And no," she smiled a fetching, lopsided smile that enhanced her already pleasing features. "I am certainly no lady. A simple farmwife from England." She sighed and rolled her eyes heavenward. Farmer's *widow*, now."

A single tear coursed its way down one cheek as her lower lip began to quiver. She took a breath to steel herself, struggled vainly not to give in to her sorrow, and began to sob.

Unable to think of what to do about this unexpected event, Thomas sat alongside her, feeling foolish and uncomfortable. *What do you say to a cryin' woman?* He wondered. His limited experience with the fairer sex left him completely at a loss. He was saved when she looked up and wiped her eyes with the back of one hand.

"I'm sorry," she said, still seeming to struggle to bring her emotions in check. Her eyes flared. "Bloody hell!" she exclaimed. "I had promised myself to be strong! Now, here I sit blubbering like a lost child!" She closed her eyes and took a deep breath. "I must be strong for my child." When she opened her eyes, she cast a measuring look in Thomas's direction. "I suppose I owe you something of an explanation." She thrust her hand in his direction and waited for him to take it in greeting. "To start with, my name is Lynn Celia Claxton." She pronounced Lynn Celia as if it were a single word, Lynncelia.

* * * *

Late the next evening, they poled their boat alongside the merchantman, *Meg,* riding at anchor between the town of Savannah and Hutchinson Island, a long, thin sliver of marshland that divided the river into two parts. It was a sturdy, if somewhat worn-looking brig, that plied the waters annually between Savannah and Portsmouth, England, carrying the annual harvest of deerskins, silk, and turpentine along with any other marketable commodities produced in the fledgling colony of Georgia. The Captain of the brig spied the boat and called a greeting to them through cupped hands.

Two ropes tumbled down from the ship. Thomas grabbed one and secured the front of the flatboat to the side of the larger vessel while one of the crewmen tied off the rear. Moments later, a crane swung out over the side and ropes were lowered for the cargo. In less than two hours it was safely stored in the cargo hold of the *Meg*.

"You've brought a fine cargo down this year, Mr. Simpson," Captain Jones complimented Richard as they sat across the table from each other. The captain had invited both men to share his supper aboard the vessel. "Here's your receipt. I trust you'll deliver it safely to your employer in the morning. We've already unloaded his consignment of trade goods." Captain Jones pushed the document across the table. "Ten thousand pounds sterling, as agreed, to be delivered in the form of trade goods on my next voyage. One pound per pound; not bad, not bad at all!" "Any trouble you know of, in town?" Richard asked.

"A young woman I brought over this year has absconded with some valuable trinkets. It's gotten your fellow colonials riled up something fierce. Half of them side with her, the other half are siding with some tavern owner she robbed." He took a long drink of steaming tea from a pewter mug and slammed it on the top of the table with a bang. "Myself, I side with the woman. She's a fine young lass who came aboard with her parents and husband 'fore we left England."

At the mention of Lynn Celia, Thomas's interest peaked. He leaned forward, resting his forearms on the table and peering intently at the captain. "We ran into the sheriff on the way down here. He asked us about this woman. What a coincidence! Can you tell us anything about her? Is there a reward?"

"Not that I know of." The captain shook his head. "Not yet, at least." He took another long drink and called for a refill. "Her parents took the ship's fever and died on the crossing. We buried them at sea. By the time we docked, her husband was fair gone too. He died about two weeks after he went ashore." He shook his head sadly. "A shame, I call it. A young woman like that, widowed in a strange land without anyone to provide for her. And her with a babe barely five months old."

"What's this about her stealing?" Thomas asked. He sat back in his chair, satisfied with what he had heard so far. It was the exact story Lynn Celia had told them the previous evening.

The captain rubbed his hand across his whiskered chin. "From what I hear, it's bunk. The tavern owner claims she wouldn't pay her bill after her husband died. He demanded a ring and a broach from her in payment before, he says, she lit out taking them with her."

"You don't believe his story?" Richard asked. He tapped Thomas on the ankle with his boot and gave him a sharp look of warning. They mustn't give themselves away with too many questions.

The captain looked from Richard to Thomas before he answered. "No, I don't. For one thing, they're goin' to auction off her trunks tomorrow at noon. That alone should settle up whatever she owes for a few nights' lodging." He smiled and nodded. "Something mighty queer about that business," he said. "For another thing, her father had title to almost two hundred acres of land just north of Ebenezer. I've still got the deed in the ship's safe. Don't know who to turn it over to."

A knowing look passed between father and son; they said nothing.

The captain waited for a moment; when no response was forthcoming, he turned up his tankard and drained it in a gulp. "Well, I think I'll turn in," he said with a nod. "You and your crew are welcome to stay aboard tonight. You can pull your boat over to the docks in the mornin'. We'll spend the day taking on fresh water and clearing with the King's revenue officer. We can be on our way the day after tomorrow."

* * * *

The following morning, they shoved off from the side of the *Meg* and steered towards the port's northernmost wharf. They tied up alongside a new structure still oozing sap and smelling of green wood. It seemed to glow a bright yellow alongside the tired gray timbers of the older wharves.

A well-dressed, middle-aged man on horseback, with a battered wooden peg protruding from the right leg of his trousers, hurried forward to meet them. The man smiled and raised his hand in a friendly salute. "Good to see you, Richard!" he said. He flashed them a good-natured smile and leaned from the saddle, offering his hand when Richard hopped from the flatboat onto the pier. Thomas could hear the sticky sound of sap on the soles of his father's boots as he stepped across the green boards.

"It's good to see you again, Morgan," Richard said with a smile. "We brought down ten thousand pounds of skins on this trip. Captain Jones was well pleased."

The other man laughed. "I suspect he was. Those skins will fetch a pretty penny for him in England—for us too." The man inclined his head in Thomas's direction. "Your mother doin' well?"

"Yes sir, Uncle Morgan," Thomas said with a quick nod.

Morgan smiled. "Good. You two stay put on the boat while your father heads over to the warehouse with me." His tone made it clear the order included Lynn Celia, who stood in the doorway of the cramped cabin. He tipped his hat to her. "You best stay out of sight, ma'am," he said quietly.

* * * *

"Morgan has arranged for our trade goods to be loaded the day after tomorrow," Richard explained when he returned. "We'll leave for Augusta the day after."

Thomas fidgeted; he seemed to be dwelling on some inner thoughts.

"What's eatin' you?" Richard asked. He smiled, guessing it had something to do with Lynn Celia even before Thomas spoke.

"What if someone recognizes her?" Thomas asked. "As pretty as she is, everyone who walks past is bound to look at her."

Richard rubbed his chin in thought. "You've got a point there."

Followed by Morgan, he stepped past his son and entered the small cabin where Lynn Celia was

23

sitting on one of the bunks, softly rubbing the back of her sleeping son.

"Mrs. Claxton," he said with a slight bob of his head, "I was just wonderin', what are your plans for the future? It's clear you can't stay in Savannah."

"I was hoping I could lay hands on my two chests at Mr. Savage's tavern. I've enough money hidden in the lining to tide me over until I can get a fresh start." She hesitated for a moment before adding, "My father also had a deed to some land in Georgia." She frowned for a moment at the memory. "He and my husband had planned on starting a farm in the colony. That's all they ever knew in England."

Richard's mouth dropped open in surprise. "Why on Earth didn't you pay off your bill, lass? It would've saved you a might of trouble."

"That wasn't the kind of payment Mr. Savage desired." Lynn Celia looked down demurely. "He didn't give me a chance to pay him, he just grabbed the only two things of value he thought I had. After that, he tried to hold poverty over me to have his way. I knew I had to get away without saying anything about the money, else he would have robbed me of it, too. Is there anything you could do to aid me?"

Morgan rubbed his chin, a frown spoiling his normally pleasant expression. "Now that's not the story we had here in town. I suspected Savage wasn't being totally honest. He's not known as a particularly upstanding citizen, in any event. More'n one poor sailor has lost his wages over to Savage's tavern." He took a deep breath and exhaled noisily. "You come with me, lass. I'll make a little visit to John Reynolds. He's the Royal Governor of the colony. We may be able to get this straightened out and put a bee in Mr. Savage's bonnet at the same time." He paused and stared at the young woman. "You best be honest about this, young lady, else you could end up like Alice Riley."

"Alice Riley?" Lynn Celia asked, puzzled.

All three of the men nodded soberly. "Alice Riley," Morgan repeated. "First woman hung in Georgia." He smiled. "Of course, she was a murderess, you're only accused of being a thief."

* * * *

Morgan Stokes led the small party to his Savannah home on the southern side of Market Place Square. Inside, he introduced Lynn Celia to his wife, Maria, who immediately took charge of

25

the disheveled woman. Maria took one look at Lynn Celia and called her maid, a rather plain-looking Spanish woman, who appeared from a side room with a feather duster in her hand. The three women, gabbing like a trio of excited hens, disappeared towards the back of the spacious home with little Roger peering wide-eyed over his mother's shoulder.

Morgan offered his two guests seats in the well-appointed sitting room. Thomas looked around appreciatively. He always found himself awed by his uncle's wealth.

His uncle caught his eye, "It still amazes me also," he said with a thin smile. "I spent my early life on the frontier, like you." He waved his hand to indicate the room. "This all came about as a result of the Indian trade. Maria and I spent several years running trading posts for Mary Musgrove. Ever hear tell of her?"

Thomas nodded. "Yes, sir. She was General Oglethorpe's interpreter during the early years of the colony."

Morgan inclined his head slightly. "And something of a cousin to you. Her father was my adopted uncle, Titus, who was killed at Bloody Marsh back in King George's War. Now that was one woman who had a head for business!" He poured himself a glass of port from an elegant glass decanter. Taking a sip, he savored its flavor for a moment before swallowing. "But she had no head at all for choosing husbands," he admitted sadly.

"Yes, sir," Thomas agreed. He had been weaned on stories about the wilder days of the colony.

Morgan pushed himself back into his chair and looked towards Richard. "Well, brother-in-law, what do you think about that pretty piece of baggage you two have picked up? Is she trustworthy?"

Thomas felt his face flush. Both of the other men saw it and exchanged glances. His Uncle Morgan smiled. "I can see what you think," he said to the young man. "It's written all over your face."

He turned his attention to his sister's husband. "What's your opinion, Richard?"

Richard rubbed his chin as he thought. "I think the girl's tellin' the truth. I already know she's been honest about the deed to that land up in Ebenezer. Captain Jones mentioned it at supper last night. There's one way to be certain, and that's to go check on those chests of hers. If there is, indeed, twenty pounds stowed in the bottom, that shoots a hole plum through Savage's story."

"Just what I was thinking myself," Morgan said. He rose abruptly. "I'm going to change into something more suitable for a visit to our distinguished governor. While Maria gets that girl..."

"Lynn Celia." Thomas interrupted.

Morgan smiled and bowed slightly to his nephew. "Lynn Celia, yes. While Maria gets Lynn Celia prepared, we'll trek over and see if we can't get this straightened out."

He gave Richard a surreptitious wink. "It's the least I can do for family. Hey, what?"

* * * *

The small party, led by Morgan, climbed the steps onto the porch of the Governor's home. Morgan adjusted his stock before rapping firmly on the door with his cane. He had dressed in his finest clothes; a well-cocked hat and a silver-tipped walking cane completed the ensemble.

The door opened. A balding, slightly built man stood staring at them for a moment before recognition crept into his eyes. "Why, Lieutenant Stokes!" he exclaimed, using Morgan's old military title, "A pleasure seeing you."

"And you." Morgan inclined his head in the man's direction. He gestured towards Richard and Thomas. "Mr. Little, these men are my brother-in-law and nephew, just arrived from Augusta with a load of skins." He introduced the man in turn. "Richard, this is Mr. William Little, the governor's secretary."

After a series of handshakes and head bobs, Mr. Little addressed Morgan. "To what do we owe the honor of your visit, sir?" There was a slight hint of perplexity in his voice. Morgan was a rare, yet welcomed, visitor at the governor's home.

Morgan inclined his head slightly in the man's direction. "Pardon my abruptness, I would have sent a note if time had permitted, but we have something of a dilemma that the governor may be able to assist us in solving. May we be permitted to talk with him for a few moments?"

Mr. Little winked. "I think I may be able to arrange that. If you gentleman would please step into the hall, I'll check with the governor."

He reappeared a few moments later and led them into a small office at the back of the house. The governor was sitting behind a mahogany desk; he held an unopened letter in one hand. He looked up and smiled. "Mr. Stokes, a pleasure to be sure." The governor stood, directing them to a semicircle of chairs stationed like silent sentinels about the front of his desk. "What brings you here? Mr. Little informs me it's something of an emergency." The governor spoke in a gruff, no-nonsense tone acquired during his years of naval service.

"Yes, sir," Morgan began. "You see, my brother-in-law has just arrived from Augusta with a load of skins. On the way downriver, he happened onto a wanted felon of yours."

The governor's eyes widened with interest. He leaned forward, intent now on Morgan's words.

Morgan smiled thinly. "It's the woman Mr. Savage is so keen to apprehend."

"Ah, yes. A thief, as I recall." The governor, an astute man, smiled. "I take it this visit has something more to it than meets the eye?"

"Yes, sir," Thomas interjected.

All three older men turned their heads to eye him. Thomas's face flushed, he cleared his throat and sat back. "Pardon me, sir," he said quietly. He glanced in Morgan's direction.

"As you see, my nephew is somewhat discombobulated about this matter. They happened on the woman yesterday and brought her downriver on their boat. She tells an interesting story." Morgan paused, waiting for the other man's response.

"And this story is?" the governor asked, one eyebrow cocked at a curious angle.

"It's this, sir." Morgan settled his back against the slats of his chair and adjusted his stock. "The woman claims she has the money to pay her bill at Mr. Savage's establishment, but he tried to have his way with her. She fled, but she claims if we search two chests she left behind, we will find twenty pounds in them, more than enough to settle her bill." Morgan paused and waited for a reaction.

The governor nodded. "Proceed."

"Mr. Savage is said to be auctioning off those chests this afternoon. If we could get an order to search them, we may be able to clear this woman's good name."

The governor leaned forward, resting his elbows on the desktop. "Tell me about this woman with a good name."

* * * *

Morgan and William Little, accompanied by two red-coated marines borrowed from a British warship in the harbor, approached Savage's Tavern. They had convinced Richard and Thomas to wait at Morgan's house, to keep what was about to happen from looking like a personal favor instead of an act of justice.

As they approached, Bill Savage gave them a wary eye from where he stood on the porch of his tavern. The two men, flanked by the marines, approached with even, steady steps. A motley crew of rivermen, sailors, and townspeople were milling about at the foot of the tavern steps, waiting for the impromptu auction to begin. They parted to let Morgan's party pass. As Savage waited, he spit a large glob of tobacco onto the ground and wiped his lips with the back of his hand.

"What can I do for your honors?" he said sourly. He gave Little and Morgan a venomous stare. His lips parted as if he intended to say more, but the sight of the two redcoats tromping at their heels gave him a hint of warning. Instead of speaking, he forced a counterfeit smile onto his lips and waited for them to ascend the steps.

Morgan's peg leg made a dull thumping sound as he crossed the boards to where Savage stood. The two men stood eye to eye. There had never been any love lost between them, and they saw no reason to pretend friendship now.

Savage shrugged his shoulders like a man preparing for a free-for-all and gave Morgan a haughty look. "Come to bid on these fine articles, is it?" he asked.

Using his cane, Little guided Savage to one side. He jabbed the silver tip at a pair of battered trunks sitting on the porch. "Actually, we've just come to have a look through those trunks."

When Savage opened his mouth to protest, Mr. Little quickly added, "At the request of the governor." Savage paused for only a moment, a flicker of warning crossed his eyes; it was quickly gone. "There's nothing in them but sundry articles of clothing, not much of value. I'm just trying to recoup some of the losses I sustained when that Claxton wench run off without payin' her bill." His words were clipped, defensive. "Ain't nothin' wrong with that, is there, Mr. Little?"

Little gave the man a slight bow and replied, "Nothing at all, sir. It's just that we must check their contents for contraband before we can allow it to be sold. These trunks did arrive from England aboard the *Meg*, did they not?"

"Er … why yes, sir. What of it?" Savage was becoming warier by the moment, sensing some unseen trap.

"Did they clear with the revenue officer?"

Savage paused and swiped a dirty hand across his chin. "I don't know, I reckon they did. 'Sides, there ain't nothin' of value in them, I already checked."

Little smiled affably. "Then we may as well check them and let you get on with your business." He motioned to one of the marines who opened the lid and stepped back. Morgan stepped forward and rummaged through the chest, shaking out each garment before laying it to one side. When the first trunk was empty, he upended it and nodded to the second marine who stepped forward smartly. The soldier pried the wooden runners from the bottom of the chest with the tip of his bayonet. Each came loose with a loud pop, followed by a series of crackling sounds. Morgan examined one piece and tossed it aside. He picked up the second and turned it over, a small hollow compartment was visible on the underside. Inside was a tight roll of pound notes held together by a piece of white thread. He tapped the runner against the base of the trunk, dislodging the notes.

He handed them to Mr. Little who unrolled and counted them. "Twenty pounds. Just as the woman claimed." He looked at Morgan with a knowing expression.

Savage blew out his breath in surprise. "Well, I'll be!" he exclaimed, "Why on earth didn't that bloody wench just pay her bill instead of hightailing it out of town? Me and the sheriff rode near fifty miles trying to cut her trail."

Little gave the tavern owner a stern look. "Why indeed, Mr. Savage? Should I tell you her story?"

Savage guffawed. "I can imagine 'tis some wild tale or other. Tain't true though, that much I can swear to. You know how a woman can exaggerate when she gets excited by some imagined wrong."

"To be sure," Little said dryly. He turned to one of the onlookers. "You, sir," he said. "Are you boarding at this establishment?" Sugar would not have melted in his mouth.

"Why yes, your honor," the man answered, hesitant to be drawn into something that did not concern him.

Little smiled to put the man at ease. "What's the charge for room and board?"

A relieved expression crossed the man's face, then disappeared as he looked towards Savage, who stood scowling at little's side.

"Why, he charges a shilling a day, your honor," the man said cautiously. He acted like he was expecting the other boarders to denounce him for some nefarious crime.

Little, his right eyebrow raised in wonder, clicked his tongue against the roof of his mouth before he spoke. "That's a little rich for this establishment I should think!" He glanced towards Savage and added, "No offense intended, I assure you." With a harrumph, he straightened to his full height and mentally calculated the bill. "For the trouble you've been put to, I'll not haggle. Also, the governor has taken a special interest in seeing this case resolved; so, let me see." He lifted his chin slightly and rolled his eyes in thought. "She was here twenty-seven days, was it?" Savage grunted and nodded.

"Good." Little smiled. "That would make her bill come to one pound, seven bob, would it not?"

"More like two pounds," Savage growled. "I did have to bury her husband's carcass."

"A very Christian thing to do, sir. I am sure she will be most grateful. Two pounds it is."

Peeling two, one-pound notes from the roll of money, he extended them to Savage. "My men will see to these chests, seeing as how the lady's bill is now paid in full." He flashed a vacant smile. "And we will withdraw your warrant. Does that please you?"

"Aye, it pleases me," Savage said. His eyes betrayed hostility, clearly this was not the outcome he had intended for Lynn Celia. "Now, if you men will be off, I'll get back to my work." He dismissed them with a curt wave of his hand and turned his scowl on the waiting crowd. "Go on, get!" he growled, shooing them away with a wave of his hands.

Little and Morgan excused themselves politely. Followed by the two marines, each bearing a chest on a shoulder, they made their way along the sandy street towards the main part of town.

Little looked at Morgan as they walked. "Your brother-in-law may want to be on his guard, Mr. Stokes. From the look in yon scoundrel's eyes, this episode may not yet be at an end."

* * * *

From the doorway of his tavern, Bill Savage eyed the departing men. He was not a particularly big man, but he was packed with more than his share of meanness. *Let them think this is over*, he thought to himself. His lips curled downward as he schemed with himself. He spotted a nefarious-looking character still hanging around the front of the tavern and motioned with a jerk of his head for him to come inside. The man smiled as he climbed the steps and disappeared into the tavern behind its disgruntled owner.

Loving Lynn Celia

CHAPTER TWO

Savannah, Georgia
April 11, 1756

Lynn Celia's hand went to her mouth when she first spied the small knot of men returning with her trunks. She took a hesitant step forward and placed her hand on the railing of the front porch for support as she watched them approach. Thomas stood behind her. His heart felt as if it would leap from his chest when she leaned forward and her hip brushed his thigh. Lynn Celia seemed to take no notice.

Morgan raised his hand in a salute. "We've something that belongs to you," he called, indicating the trunks with a wave of his hand.

"I can't believe my eyes!"

"Nor I," he replied. "I almost didn't recognize you. My wife has transformed the caterpillar into a butterfly!"

Maria and her maid had wasted no time in preparing a bath and finding suitable clothing for Lynn Celia. The sun glinted off her hair, now washed and combed like a bright halo. Though she wore the black dress of a widow, they had, by far, transformed her into one of the most attractive women in Savannah.

Lynn Celia blushed. "Why, thank you, sir. That is the first compliment I have received since landing in the colonies."

Morgan smirked. "I am confident you'll get more." He gave Thomas a searching look. "Don't you think so Thomas?" he asked, giving the youth a playful elbow to the ribs.

William Little climbed onto the porch behind Morgan and gave Lynn Celia a courtly bow. "Where may we put your things, mi-lady?" His gaze stayed on her face as he waited for her to answer; he looked totally enchanted.

Maria answered for her. "If you two gentlemen will follow me," she said to the two marines, "I'll show you to the room." With that, she turned and led them into the house.

Morgan wiped his brow with a handkerchief. "I do believe I've worked up a sweat," he said to the other men. "Let's have a seat and cool off a bit." He looked at Maria's maid. "Jessica, could you fetch us some refreshments, please?"

As they waited for their drinks, the men sat in rocking chairs, enjoying a soft breeze coming off the river. They rose to their feet when Maria and Lynn Celia reappeared a few moments later.

Morgan thanked the marines and gave each of them a shilling. Their eyes lit up like twin lanterns as they thanked him and marched away. That was two days' pay to them.

After refreshments were served, the conversation turned to Lynn Celia's future.

"What are your plans?" William Little asked.

She paused a moment before admitting she was at a loss as just what to do.

"If I may be so bold as to advise you," he said. "Wouldn't it be wise for one of us to take a boat out to the *Meg* and retrieve the deed to your land? The ship does sail with the morning tide."

"Excellent suggestion!" Morgan agreed. He turned to Thomas. "Would you be so kind as to retrieve the document for the lady?"

Before Thomas could answer, Lynn Celia came up with a suggestion of her own. "Would it not be better if I accompanied him? The captain may require a signature and a receipt."

Thomas felt as if he were the luckiest man in the world. His face beamed, a fact that was not lost on any of the other people on the porch.

* * * *

Loving Lynn Celia

After nursing Roger and consigning him to Jessica's care, Lynn Celia set off for the *Meg* with Thomas. In a happy daze, he walked at Lynn Celia's side. He kept turning his head to look at her as she spoke; she had to warn him twice when he would have tripped and once more when he was about to step into one of the steaming mounds of horse apples littering the Savannah street.

They were able to hire one of the many skiffs on the waterfront to row them to the *Meg* and wait while they conducted their business with Captain Jones. The three of them sat around the table in the captain's cabin as he drew up a receipt for the contents in the ship's safe.

"One more thing, Mrs. Claxton," the captain said as he pressed his ring to the wax seal on the document, "there is also this." He held out a sealed envelope with her husband's name on it. "I have no idea what it contains. You may open it if you wish, or take it with you to peruse later."

Lynn Celia folded the letter and placed it in her apron pocket along with the deed. "I think I'll wait until I'm alone," she answered quietly.

"Of course." The captain agreed. He stood and said, "If you will permit me, I must take my leave. There is much to do before we sail tomorrow."

G.G. Stokes, Jr.

* * * *

They were halfway to the dock when Thomas first noticed the three disreputable men standing at the base of the bluff. Lynn Celia saw them too; she reached out and discreetly squeezed Thomas's forearm.

"Looks like trouble," the boatman said dryly. "You two best watch out." He surreptitiously reached into the bottom of the skiff and slipped a wood-handled boning knife into Thomas's hand. "Best tuck this into your trousers young man. Unless I miss my guess, those three are up to no good. Wish I could help, but…" He shrugged his shoulders and spread his bony arms to display his emaciated form. "They'd chew me up and spit me out before you could say *spit*. Want me to take you to one of the piers farther down?"

Thomas, more worried for Lynn Celia's welfare than his own, looked right and left. It was suppertime. A few workmen were making repairs to one of the docks on the south end, but other than them, the strand was all but deserted. Thomas noted with a sinking feeling in the pit of his stomach that his father's flatboat was also deserted. The crew was no doubt scattered about taverns from one end of Savannah to the other.

"No," he told the boatman. "Put us on the new pier to the north, across from my father's flatboat." Thomas jabbed a finger in the direction of the boat.

The boatman expertly rowed the craft to the spot indicated, where it thumped against one of the pilings as it came to a rest. Keeping the craft pulled snugly alongside the pier with one hand, he helped Lynn Celia out of the unstable craft with the other, then held the boat steady while Thomas disembarked. He wasted no time in pushing off. Using his paddle as a rudder, he steered downriver. He looked back once and waved his hand in a sad farewell as he drifted away on the current.

Thomas took a deep breath and rubbed his hand over the knife handle protruding from the waist of his breeches. He took a few tentative steps along the pier, then, holding Lynn Celia's hand, leaped onto the flatboat and jumped into the cabin. He slammed the door and barred it.

After pulling his father's blunderbuss from under the bed, he swung a window open and confronted the three men thundering toward them. All three men came to an abrupt halt when Thomas pulled the hammer to full cock and pointed the bell-shaped barrel directly at them.

"I would stop right there, unless you want a belly full of nails and buckshot," he advised them.

One of the men wiped his mouth with the back of his hand and presented him with a gap-toothed smile. "What's eatin' you youngin'? We're just three poor fishermen, out lookin' for a job. We thought you and your lady might be able to steer us in the right direction." The three men continued to sidle towards the flatboat as he spoke.

Thomas thrust the barrel of the blunderbuss a few inches in their direction. "Best be on your way Mr. Fisherman," he quipped. "Like I said, the only thing you're likely to catch around here is a belly full of rusty iron."

A dull thump on the end of the pier, followed by the slapping sounds of bare feet padding on boards, caught the attention of the three men. Their faces paled as they turned and scurried off the end of the pier. Thomas watched as they bounded across the sandy strand and raced up the steps to the top of the bluff, where they disappeared in the direction of Barnard Street. A half dozen sailors in slops passed the window at a run and pursued them into town.

"I thought you may need a hand." Captain Jones's voice called from the pier. Thomas stuck his head out of the window and spied the mariner standing on the dock just aft of the flatboat. He was leaning on a cutlass, using it as a cane.

"You thought correctly, sir!" Thomas answered. He eased the hammer of the blunderbuss to half cock and leaned it against the cabin wall. Taking a pale-faced Lynn Celia by the hand, he led her out onto the deck. "I can't thank you enough," he said to the captain.

The captain bellowed good-naturedly. "My pleasure. One of my men spotted that gang of cutthroats from the ship. We could tell by the look of 'em they were up to no good. Our only fear was that we would not reach you in time. Good thinkin', coming ashore near your flatboat. If it hadn't been for that…" he shook his head. "Let's just say it would not have been a pretty sight." He tapped the butt of a brass-handled pistol visible beneath his coat. "Between this pistol and your blunderbuss, I think we can make it to your uncle's home unmolested." He sheathed his cutlass and cocked his arm in invitation. "Come now, Mrs. Claxton," he said. "The two of us will see you safely home."

* * * *

Morgan listened, incredulous at the tale of Thomas and Lynn Celia's narrow escape. He pounded his fist on the table, causing the wine glasses and trays to chatter fretfully. "The insolence of the man!" he roared. Red-faced with anger, he surveyed the three fugitives. "I'll have that swine thrown into jail this very night!" he declared.

"Let's not be too hasty, Mr. Stokes," William Little interjected. "There is no proof it was Mr. Savage who arranged this ambuscade." He looked at Captain Jones. "Captain, what do you think? You were there; a ship's captain with a good eye." With a hasty smile, he added, "To the relief of us all."

Captain Jones cleared his throat as he thought about his reply. Unconsciously, he ran his finger around the inside of his stock, feeling the stubble sprouting beneath it. "It's hard to say, sir," he said. "The men looked like common riffraff. It could have very well been a coincidence that it happened today of all days." He took a deep breath before adding, "If my men happen to catch one of the buggers though…"

"Quite right," Little agreed. He looked at Thomas. "Are you certain you could recognize them if you were to see them again?"

"Perfectly certain, sir," Thomas answered without hesitation. "If you would like, I could go to Mr. Savage's tavern. If they're there, I could point them out."

Little dismissed the suggestion with a wave of his hand. "No need to move so hastily," he cautioned. "If they are confederates of Mr. Savage, they'll know they were recognized. It would be foolish of them to return there."

"I hate to agree, but that does make sense," Morgan said with a disgusted twist of his lips. He looked at Thomas. "Lad," he said with a grin, "you might check with the women and make certain Mrs. Claxton is not too overwrought by this incident. A rather frightening event if I say so myself."

After Thomas had stepped out of the room, and Morgan was certain his voice would not carry to the women upstairs, he looked at the other three men sitting around his table. His gaze fastened on his brother-in-law. "Richard, I would wager a month's profits Savage was behind this. But unless we have some proof, English law protects him." He paused and took a sip of port. "You'll be leaving in a few days with Thomas. That will put the two of you out of danger in any event. What do you three gentlemen think we should do to safeguard Mrs. Claxton?"

"She does have two hundred acres of land upriver from Ebenezer," Little said. "Without a doubt, there are many able-bodied men in the colony who would be willing to marry her. In that case, I am certain she would not be molested."

Morgan harrumphed. "That land can't be more than twenty miles from here. If she settles on it, and Savage and his cronies should find out where she is, she and her new husband would find themselves living among many dangerous enemies." He studied the contents of his wine glass for a moment before gulping it down. "She would be in as much peril there as she is here."

Captain Jones volunteered an answer, "Charleston?"

"We would like to keep her in our little colony if possible," Little reminded the other men. "After years of utopia at the hands of the trustees, we are almost devoid of citizens and wealth. Governor Reynolds will not look kindly on us sending our new arrivals to South Carolina. There's already been talk of our friends to the north absorbing Georgia into their own colony."

"What about Augusta?" Richard asked. "The woman was reared on a farm, she would be useful there until she caught the eye of some man who would provide for her."

"What about me?" All four men started slightly at the unexpected voice from the staircase. They turned and craned their necks to see Thomas standing halfway down the steps. Lynn Celia was beside him, and Maria, flanked by Jessica, stood behind.

Lynn Celia's eyelashes fluttered. Surprise crossed her face. "You don't mean that Thomas," she said with a sad smile. "I'm a twenty-two-year-old widow with a child. You're what? Seventeen?"

"Eighteen." Thomas corrected her.

"Well, yes, you do look much older," she said to placate him. "But that still makes me twenty-two."

"What does age matter? I can run a farm as well as any man, I'm sure you can do the household chores better'n most women. Why, it's high time I struck out on my own." Thomas felt his face flush when he noticed the condescending looks of the men at the table. Lynn Celia felt his embarrassment. She laid her hand on his forearm.

"On second thought," she said, "let's wait and see what the future brings. When we get to know each other better..." She raised an eyebrow provocatively and smiled, displaying even white teeth. The others in the room took their cue from her and eagerly seconded the idea.

"Maybe, when your time of mourning for your husband is over, you'll change your mind?" Thomas said hopefully.

"Oh? But I'm not mourning for my husband," Lynn Celia said with a reassuring pat on his forearm.

Loving Lynn Celia

CHAPTER THREE

Savannah, Georgia
April 12, 1756

Conscious of the shocked looks directed at her by her hosts, Lynn Celia quickly explained herself. "You must understand, I had great respect for my husband and he was a wonderful man, but my marriage was not a love match, it was arranged by my family. That's why I would prefer to wait. I hope my next marriage will be to a man I truly love.

Several frowns stared up at her from below; this would not be a popular position in this society. Allowing Thomas to take her arm, she followed him down the stairs and claimed a vacant chair next to the fireplace. An awkward silence ensued. She looked at the four men arranged around the table. "Am I to understand that honesty is not valued in Georgia?" she asked with a wiry smile. The men sat, completely at a loss for words.

Richard Simpson broke the silence. "Why no, ma'am," he replied. "It's just that we are somewhat taken aback by it in this case. Please excuse our, er … our reticence."

"You are excused," Lynn Celia said, exonerating the men of their duty to make further statements. She took in a large breath and exhaled it in one fell swoop. "Now! As for my future. I realize it may be frowned upon for a woman to take up land by herself, but I am most anxious to get on with my life." She looked directly at William Little and continued, "What would be the reaction to my taking on a hired man?"

The four men at the table exchanged dubious glances. Little thought for a moment before he answered. "It would depend on the man. An older, married man with his wife along? That would be tolerated. A younger, single man? That would raise more than a few eyebrows and set loose tongues to wagging."

Lynn Celia threw back her head and looked down her nose at him. "Where would I find such a man?"

Little grinned waggishly. "You wouldn't," he replied. "Any man in that position would be taking up his own land."

"So you're saying. I either give up my land or marry to keep it?"

"Ideally, if not legally." Little pursed his lips. "I must be totally honest with you, Mrs. Claxton. Legally, you may own land as a widow in this colony. Practically though, that is an entirely different matter. May I make a suggestion?"

"Please do."

"If you want to remain unmarried, sell the land you've just inherited and buy a town lot. You could support yourself here in any number of occupations without the risk to your life that the frontier offers."

"Support myself how? As a spinster?"

"That is one possibility."

Lynn Celia compressed her lips into a straight line and pouted for a few moments. Her eyes swung to Thomas. "Would you escort me onto the verandah?" she cooed. "All of this is a bit overwhelming. I feel a pressing need to clear my head with some fresh air."

Thomas dutifully extended his arm.

"Just hold on one moment!" Both Morgan and Captain Jones objected at the same time. Morgan rose from his seat, disapproval etched on every feature of his face. "Are the two of you daft?" he stammered. "You've just escaped with your lives from a pack of rogues, and you want to step out into the darkness, unguarded?"

"But the four of you are here," Lynn Celia objected sweetly. "You could be outside in only a moment if I hailed you. Couldn't you?"

A vexed expression crossed Morgan's face. His cheeks turned faintly pink. He bowed stiffly, defeated. "By all means, take your air. We four will be ready to assist you at a moment's notice."

Once on the porch, out of earshot of the others, Lynn Celia turned to Thomas. "I have a proposition for you. I am not ready to marry again, it wouldn't be proper. Would you be willing to work for me on my land?"

"Why … yes," Thomas stammered. "Didn't I make that clear? I *was* asking to marry you."

Lynn Celia furrowed her brows. "That's not what I'm asking. I'm asking if you would be willing to work for wages, or for a part of the profit from my land."

Thomas looked keenly disappointed. "You're turning me down?"

Lynn Celia's lower lip quivered slightly. "Yes, at least for now. If you'll come and help me get settled, I'll think about it." Before a smile could grace the young man's face, she added, "I'm not promising anything, other than I'll think about it."

"For how long?"

"One year," she stated. "I will either marry you one year from today or dissolve our partnership. Is it a deal?"

Thomas couldn't hold his emotions in check. He reached out and pulled her to him, enveloping her in his arms. She looked past his shoulder as he patted her gently on the back. A tear slid down her cheek.

It took the better part of the night to wring an agreement out of Thomas's father and uncle; William Little never wholeheartedly embraced the idea. Captain Jones departed early with a farewell to his ex-passenger and the other members of the household. He would be back in England within three months at the most. He offered to return Lynn Celia to any family still in Wiltshire, but she refused, explaining she was tentatively betrothed and would not go back on her word.

* * * *

The next morning, Thomas and Lynn Celia stepped out together and strolled through the town market; there were many things to buy before leaving in the morning. As an early wedding present, Uncle Morgan had given Thomas the old dog lock musket he had carried twenty-odd years ago in the colony's war with the Spaniards. Although almost thirty years old, it was still in excellent shape. Thomas admired the graceful curve of the French-style stock. The fact that the stock had been cut back from the muzzle so a bayonet could be affixed would hold him in good stead when he attended drills with the militia.

As they entered one store near the end of the market, Lynn Celia gasped; her hand went to her throat. "Oh, look, Thomas!" she said. Pointing to a well-made spinning wheel sitting in one corner, she smiled like a little girl. The wheel looked used, but not abused. When she ran her hand over it, it seemed more of a caress than an appraisal.

"I wonder how much this is?" she thought out loud.

The owner, a balding, pudgy man, was busy stocking the shelves with colorful cloth prints newly arrived from England. He stopped and looked over his shoulder. "Why ma'am, I'll take five pounds for that. I just picked it up the other day. A woman who arrived from England aboard the *Meg* died two days ago." He made a vague motion towards the harbor with one hand. "The sheriff sold it to me in order to raise money to support her daughter until the poor thing can be sent down to Bethesda."

"Bethesda?" Lynn Celia's expression clearly indicated this was an unknown place.

"The orphan's home, down south of the city," the merchant explained.

"Do you remember the woman's name?" Lynn Celia asked, more than a hint of dread evident in her voice.

The merchant scratched his head, flicked his tongue across his lips, and rubbed his chin, but seemed unable to recall the name. He shook his head. "No, ma'am. Though, if I recall correctly, the girl's about eight or nine."

"Where would I find the sheriff?" Lynn Celia snapped, impatient to be off.

"Courthouse square, more'n likely," the man answered. "You still want the spinning wheel? It's a mere four pounds."

"Sir," Lynn Celia said flatly, "you keep that wheel right where it is until I get back and I'll give you two pounds sterling for it."

"Three."

"Two pounds, ten. Take it or leave it."

The man rubbed his head as he mulled it over. "It's too early in the mornin' to be robbed," he said, chuckling to make certain his statement wasn't perceived as an insult. "In that case, good day, sir." Lynn Celia's reply was short and clipped.

As she turned to go, the man relented. "Just to keep my wife from leaving me for being such a fool, would you consider two pounds, three?"

Lynn Celia made a great pretense of struggling inwardly, knowing all the while she would die if she didn't get the wheel, it was exactly what she was looking for. "Let's split the difference," she relented, "two pounds, two, and 6 pence."

The merchant hesitated and seemed about to suffer an apoplexy before nodding. "Aye. Its highway robbery, but I want to find a good home for it. When will you be back to pick it up?"

* * * *

"Where're you goin' so fast?" Thomas asked as he stepped along at Lynn Celia's side. She was moving along Barnard Street at a brisk pace, little puffs of dry sand erupted from beneath her feet with each step.

"I'm going to check on that orphan!" she declared between gulps of air.

"Do you know her?"

"She's a little girl who came over with me on the *Meg*. Her mother was a widow from Wiltshire, bound to wed a settler at some place called Sunbury."

Thomas reached out and grabbed her arm. He stopped, pulling her to an abrupt halt alongside him. "How do you know it's the same girl?"

She spun to face him. "Let me go, Thomas!" Her voice was an urgent whisper. "It can't be anyone else, there was only one girl that age on the *Meg*. I can't leave her alone in a strange country. She must be scared unto death!"

Thomas gave her a searching look. He nodded. "Come on, we'll go together, but for God's sake, slow down! You act like you're on fire."

Percival Square, more commonly called Courthouse Square, was located at the rear of the town, away from the hubbub and confusion of the riverfront. Thomas and Lynn Celia arrived at the courthouse just in time to see a small child lifted into the back of a two-wheeled cart by the sheriff. Thomas hailed him as he and Lynn Celia rushed across the dusty square. The sheriff stood with open curiosity, watching them approach.

"Thank God we made it in time!" Thomas panted. "We thought we'd be too late to stop you from sending the child to Bethesda."

The sheriff studied Thomas's face for a moment. "Don't I know you?" he asked.

"Yes, sir," Thomas responded. "I saw you on the river a few days ago."

"Ah! Yes. I remember now, you were on a flatboat." He gave them an appraising look, seemed to find them acceptable, and nodded his head. "You kin to this girl?"

"I am her godmother," Lynn Celia explained. "I came over on the *Meg* with her and I promised her mother I would take the child as my own should anything happen to her."

The sheriff eyed her dubiously. "You have papers to that effect?"

Lynn Celia hesitated; a hint of indecision crossed her face. "No, sir..." she stammered. "But does a promise need to be in writing to be kept?"

"Legally it does." He looked up at the driver. "William, hold up a mite, I need to question these people before we leave." He shifted his gaze back to Thomas. "Come with me," he said in a gruff voice. "I'll see what I can do." He motioned for them to follow him to the town jail.

Behind them, the girl looked over the high-sided cart. Recognizing Lynn Celia, she let out a squeal of joy and jumped from the back of the cart. Lynn Celia knelt and scooped her into her arms as they both burst into tears. The sheriff motioned again for them to follow.

In the jail, he pointed out two battered chairs for them to sit in. Lynn Celia sat with Patience on her lap. Her eyes followed the sheriff's every move. "Is there going to be a legal problem?" she asked in a fretful voice.

The sheriff said, "There very well could be." He seated himself behind his desk and rested both elbows on top, surveying both of them for a long moment. "How long have the two of you been married?" He gave them a sympathetic smile. "Newlyweds by the look of you."

"We're not married sir, only betrothed," Thomas admitted shyly.

"If it's a matter of money for her board, I'll gladly pay it." Lynn Celia said quickly. She looked from the sheriff to Thomas, then back.

"There's more to it than that. Reverend Whitfield has a passion for collecting orphans so he can train them in the ways of the Lord. He will kick his heels loud and high if I let him lose one to a young couple that ain't even wed." He eyed Patience for a moment before continuing. "I've no doubt you would give the girl a good home, but I'm sorry miss, unless you're married, no judge is going to let you have an orphan child.

Especially with the good Reverend whispering into his ear and arguing for her soul."

The sheriff rose to go. He hesitated for a moment when Patience and Lynn Celia both burst into renewed fits of sobbing. Taking his hat from the desk, he bowed slightly. "I'll give the two of you a few moments to say goodbye," he said quietly before leaving the room.

Lynn Celia looked at Thomas, who stood, clearly befuddled, beside her chair. "What can we do?" She sniffed. "Can't Mr. Little or the governor do anything?"

"I'm sure they could, but there's no time. Maybe we could…"

They were interrupted by the return of the sheriff. A tall, somber man entered behind him. They both removed their hats. "This is the child, Reverend Whitfield." The sheriff held out a hand to Patience. "Come girl, it's time to be leavin'." His voice had a touch of melancholy in it.

"Please!" Lynn Celia pleaded. Tears streamed down her face as she clutched Patience to her breast. Her heartbroken expression begged for more time. The two men hesitated, taken aback at the pure passion behind her plea.

The sheriff cleared his throat. He looked to the reverend and explained. "These two want to adopt the child. It seems miss…" He gave Lynn Celia a questioning look.

"Claxton," Lynn Celia said through her tears. "Lynn Celia Claxton."

The sheriff's eyes flared in recognition of the name, his lips parted slightly as if to speak, then snapped shut as he thought better of it. He cleared his throat again and continued talking to Reverend Whitfield. "It seems Mrs. Claxton had promised the child's mother she would care for her if anything happened to her. She seems very keen on carrying out her vow."

The reverend took a deep breath. With a scowl, he stared down the bridge of his nose, surveying the heartbroken woman. "I take it there is some legal concern over that arrangement?"

"Yes, sir. She and Mr..." He looked towards Thomas.

"Simpson."

"Mr. Simpson, are betrothed, but not married. That being the case, I don't think the court will award them custody." He shrugged and waited for the reverend's response.

"I see..." the reverend drawled. He looked at Thomas. "When is this marriage to take place?"

Thomas cleared his throat and shuffled his feet. "A year from today," he admitted sheepishly.

"Oh, my! That is a problem," the reverend opined. He looked back to Lynn Celia. "I'm sorry, miss, but that being the case, I had better take the child with me. I can see your earnestness, but a

65

year? I'm sorry. That is much too long. A lot can happen in a year."

A look of pure defeat crossed her face; Lynn Celia slumped back in her chair and hugged Patience even tighter. The child looked up, their eyes met and suddenly Lynn Celia found herself on her feet, looking expectantly at the solemn-faced minister. "Reverend Whitlock, what if we married?" she said, "Now, today?"

CHAPTER FOUR

New Ebenezer, Georgia
April 16, 1756

Thomas sat up in his blankets and yawned. He looked down at the sleeping form of his wife and rubbed his fingertips along the curve of her hip. She lay on her side with her back to him. Across from them, on one of the other cramped bunks in the flatboat cabin, Patience slept with her arms around Lynn Celia's snoring infant. *A ready-made family*, his father had called them when they had returned to his Uncle Morgan's home with Patience in tow and broken the news to him that he had a new daughter in the family—and two unexpected grandchildren.

He shook his wife's shoulder; she stirred and looked up sleepy-eyed.

"Time to get up lazy bones," he teased, "if you're still bent on cookin' us some breakfast before the sun comes up."

He leaned over and kissed her on the temple. She brushed her hands across her face, sighed, kicked off the blanket, and rolled out of bed. She paused long enough to pull the heavy wool blanket back over Thomas and pat him on the shoulder.

"You get some more rest," she said quietly. "I'll make breakfast for the crew.

* * * *

They pushed off as soon as it grew light enough to see. It was a cool morning that drew wisps of fog from the warm current of the river. Lynn Celia sat on top of the small cabin with Roger resting in her lap. She whiled away the hours watching the slow, methodical rhythm of the boatmen as they set their poles at the front of the boat and walked them to the rear, only to turn around and follow the inside walkway back to the bow where they would reset the pole and begin their steady push once again. Over and over, the cycle was repeated as the men fought against the current. It would take three weeks to pole upriver to Augusta.

Lynn Celia pulled the letter Captain Jones had given her from her apron pocket. She studied it for a moment before slipping her finger beneath the seal and opening it. Her lips moved slightly as she read to herself. She looked up, a puzzled expression on her face.

"What is it?" Thomas asked with concern. He couldn't take his eyes off of her as he walked his pole forward. She held the letter out to him; he shook his head. "Can't stop now. Is it important?"

"I would say, yes."

Thomas looked towards his father who was standing at the bow, watching the river ahead for any debris coming from upriver. If a drifting log slipped beneath the bow of the boat, it could upset the whole craft and lead to disaster.

His father looked over his shoulder as if some sixth sense were at work between them. "I'll take a turn on the walkway," he volunteered. "I could use a little exercise."

Thomas walked to the bow and transferred the smooth pole to his father. He clambered onto the roof of the cabin and knelt beside his wife. She offered the letter to him again. He hesitated a moment, rubbing his hand on the side of his breeches. He took the letter and looked at her apologetically. It was Lynn Celia's turn to ask what was wrong.

"I can't read," he admitted. He thrust the letter back at her, red-faced with embarrassment.

"Nothing to be ashamed of," she consoled him, "most folks can't."

"What's it say?"

"It's to my…" She caught herself before saying *my husband*. "It's to Roger's father.

It seems there's a man in New Ebenezer, a German he met when we stopped over in Charleston. He is offering to trade three hundred acres between Augusta and a place in South Carolina called Ninety-Six. It's on the Cherokee Path." She looked up. "Do you know of it?"

A wide grin split Thomas's face. "I know exactly where it is. They just opened up that land last year after the treaty with the Cherokee." Noting the puzzled look on his wife's face, Thomas explained. "The Cherokee are a tribe up north of here. One of the two most powerful in this area. Last year, they signed away a sight of land in South Carolina."

"Is it good land?"

"Much better than this." He waved his hand along the shoreline to indicate the area. "This land is not healthy; it breeds fever. And the mosquitoes? In the summer, they'll eat you alive!"

"You think we should take him up on his offer?"

Thomas nodded. "Yes, I do. But let's go talk with this German fella before we make up our minds. Does the letter give his name and where he lives?"

* * * *

Two days later, Lynn Celia and Thomas dismounted from their borrowed mounts in a small clearing twenty miles north of New Ebenezer. It was a spot Thomas knew well. It was often used as a layover for flatboat crews heading up the river from Savannah.

After exchanging farewells with the burly German who had exchanged deeds with them, they handed over the reins of their borrowed mounts and watched him disappear back down the narrow trail.

That evening, with Roger riding papoose fashion on Lynn Celia's back, they scrambled aboard the flatboat when it came ashore. Patience, who had remained aboard, leaped into Lynn Celia's arms, jubilant at her return.

"Did you make the trade?" his father asked as soon as the boat was tied up.

Thomas held up the paper. "Sure did. Three hundred acres just this side of Ninety-six with a spring-fed stream runnin' right through the middle of it. We couldn't of asked for a better place."

"Why'd he want to get rid of it?"

"Scared of Indians." Thomas laughed. "Lucky for us, huh?"

Richard smiled his agreement. "Come on." He jerked his head towards the forest on the south side of the river. "Let's go get some firewood for Lynn Celia. We near starved half to death eatin' our own cookin' again."

They had just sat down to a dinner of johnnycakes and salt pork when a voice hailed them from upriver. A boat coming from Augusta was edging towards the south bank with the intention of tying up alongside them. A large, rough-looking man stood at the bow waving his battered hat in greeting.

Richard waved them to the shore. "Welcome, Wallace!" he called back. "I hope you have some hard money this time. We were just talkin' up a game of checkers for after supper."

The other man laughed good-naturedly and shook his head. "I always counsel my men to keep their money well hidden whenever we sleep over with that bunch of cutthroats you call a crew."

Richard's entire crew erupted in laughter. They knew Wallace's men well, were related to them in many cases. The two captains shook hands warmly.

"A might late comin' down, ain't you?" Richard asked.

"I'm fair certain we're the last boat this season. It's startin' to get too hot for good skins." Leaving his crew to secure the flatboat, he ambled over to the fire and plopped down onto a log. Its top had been worn smooth by the rear end of many a boatman in the past. Lynn Celia held out a mug of tea. He accepted with a nod. His eyes held a question that his lips did not ask.

"Wallace," Richard said, taking a seat alongside him, "this here's my new daughter-in-law, Lynn Celia. Thomas wed her in Savannah, just before we started back upriver."

Wallace gave her a quick bob of the head. "Pleased to meet you, ma'am." He rolled his eyes in Richard's direction. "That son of yours can really pick 'em, I'd say."

Richard gave Lynn Celia an appraising look and nodded. "He did right well for himself." Lynn Celia blushed at the compliment. She stood and brushed the brown leaves of last autumn from her skirt, excused herself, and headed to the flatboat cabin.

Inside the cabin, she sat on her bunk, cradling Roger in her lap, her blouse open to him. He made greedy sounds as he attacked her breast with relish. Patience and Thomas sat opposite her, talking together of the day's events and planning their future. Outside, around the fire, the boatmen would periodically erupt into boisterous rounds of laughter. Someone began to scratch out a tune on a fiddle. A fife joined in. They were playing *Brighten Camp*. As the tempo increased, a slight smile graced Lynn Celia's features; she tapped her foot in time to the rhythm and grinned in Thomas's direction. "Do you like to dance?"

"I do a mighty fine hornpipe, if I say so myself," Thomas replied. He straightened his back and puffed out his chest. "You may not know it, but you married yourself one hell of a fine dancer." He inclined his head to indicate Roger. "You let that little pig finish emptyin' the trough, and we'll take a step or two together." He grinned back at her; it was more of a challenge than anything else. Lynn Celia beamed. She studied his face in the flickering firelight coming through the window of the cabin. They were an odd couple, already married with two children to raise, but just getting to know each other.

Lynn Celia swung the baby from one breast to the other. "I might just take you up on that Mr. Simpson," she said. Her face was lost in the shadows of the cabin, but Thomas could imagine her crooked smile directed towards him.

"I'm warnin' you, you best be prepared to sleep well tonight Mrs. Simpson. You'll be worn down to a nubbin' when I get through with you." Thomas turned his attention to Patience. He ruffled her hair, setting her mobcap askew. She gave him one of her best snaggle-toothed smiles. "What you smilin' at little bit?" He grinned. "I may start on you after I've danced Lynn Celia into the ground."

Leaving Roger resting comfortably on the bunk, Lynn Celia allowed Thomas to drag her by the hand from the cabin. They jumped onto the bank and sauntered into the circle of firelight. Without hesitation, Thomas launched into a wild hornpipe as the fiddlers stepped up the tempo and the fifes shrilled along. It only took a moment for others to join them. Burley boatmen danced together in careless abandon; smiles and catcalls abounded. Those watching beat time with their hands and feet.

At the insistence of Lynn Celia, an English country dance followed, with unequal lines that ensured she and Patience would dance up and down the line with a different partner each time. The men grinned like children, enamored by this small, dark-haired Englishwoman who had so suddenly become a part of their close-knit community.

Lynn Celia was careful to keep an eye on Patience as the young girl danced along the line. For the first time since she and Thomas had plucked the child from the back of the cart in

Savannah, she seemed to be smiling wholeheartedly. One of the boatmen, a French Canadian exile from Acadia, seemed to be her favorite partner. The older man treated her like a miniature woman, praising her dancing ability in his heavily accented English each time the dancers took a break.

With much singing and cavorting, the party lasted well into the night. The two captains bowed to the public outcry and broke open a small keg of rum. Conscious of tomorrow's work, they rationed it out, allowing each man only one pint—and that watered down. Wallace proposed a toast to the bride and groom. The men roared their approval when Lynn Celia demanded a tankard of the brew and downed it in a salute to her own wedding. Even Patience was allowed one sip; she screwed up her face in distaste of the foul-tasting liquid.

At the insistence of the two captains, the men turned in at midnight. They spread their blankets in a circle, their feet to the fire, and settled down. Soon, snores replaced the quiet murmur of voices. Away in the night, the wildlife of the river seemed to increase its own noises as those of the intruders died down. Frogs and crickets chirped in a discordant symphony; a bull alligator roared defiance somewhere in the darkness.

Hand in hand, Thomas and Lynn Celia made their way back to the flatboat where they transferred the snoring Roger to the spare bunk. Thomas was taken aback when his wife whispered to Patience and led her out of the cabin. He could hear their soft words as Lynn Celia made a bed on top of one of the crates of trade goods and tucked the child in. She slipped silently back into the cabin, slid the glass of the candle lantern up, and blew on the taper; darkness immediately claimed the cabin. With more than a bit of trepidation, he listened to the soft rumpling of her skirts as she undressed and lay her clothes alongside the sleeping child on the far bunk. She slid onto the bed alongside him and burrowed against his side. When he did not move, she lifted his arm and draped it around her shoulders. With a start, Thomas realized she was naked. In his life this was something new, most women never disrobed farther than their shifts.

"Lynn Celia," Thomas said in a trembling voice. "I have a confession to make." She snuggled closer and looked up, studying the outline of his face in the darkness.

"What is it?"

He hesitated and looked down. "I ain't never done this before."

"That makes it even better," she whispered. She reached up and began to loosen the drawstring at the neck of his shirt. "Come on," she whispered, "I'll show you how."

The next morning, Thomas poled with renewed vigor. His head spun at the thought of last night. The marriage had now been consummated—twice! It was now legal in the eyes of the church and the law. It would last as long as he and Lynn Celia lived. He shook his head at the thought, both happy and unbelieving at God's grace in guiding him to the woman he would spend the remainder of his life with. It was a good feeling, he wished he could share it with someone. He smiled as he realized that he could—with Lynn Celia.

Thomas felt his happiness would last forever; he believed his mother would find as much joy in his marriage as he did. But as with everything in life, disappointment often follows high hopes.

CHAPTER FIVE

Augusta, Georgia
May 7, 1756

Thomas was troubled. Since they had arrived in Augusta, his mother's attitude towards Lynn Celia had been distinctly cold. He couldn't understand it.

"It ain't seemly, Richard," he overheard her telling his father one night when they thought everyone was asleep. "That woman's husband ain't been dead two months and she's already wed our Thomas. What do you think she'll do if anything ever happens to him?" She blew out her breath in exasperation. "It ain't seemly, I tell you. There's something wrong with a woman who'll throw off her husband's memory so handily. You don't reckon she's with child and lookin' for a man, do you?" He heard his father's low voice answer all the charges. It ended in an angry exchange. It was obvious he and his new bride could not stay in his parents' house for any length of time and expect to live in peace.

Lynn Celia boldly told him the following morning it was time for them to move onto their South Carolina land, even if it meant living in a fly tent until they were able to erect a cabin. After much arguing and cajoling, Thomas convinced her to stay with his sister while he and three of his brothers went to survey the land and put up a cabin. He also pointed out that dragging a small child through the wilderness was just asking for trouble. Faced with the possibility her child could suffer, Lynn Celia relented and agreed to stay behind.

Three days later, leading two packhorses loaded with tools and supplies, the four men set out. It was a short, uneventful two days.

Six miles southwest of the small village of Ninety-Six, South Carolina, they happened on the landmarks the old German had described to Thomas. The land lay level, bordered to the west by a shallow swamp held back by a large beaver dam. A half-mile farther on, a clear, gushing spring, no more than fifty yards off the main trail, produced a shallow stream that meandered through an idyllic natural meadow covered with a thick blanket of yellow broom straw that made soft, swishing sounds as it waved to and fro in response to gentle puffs of wind coming out of the northwest.

Thomas reined in his mount and sat admiring his new home in open-mouthed wonder. He simply shook his head, unable to fully comprehend that this was now his land. Still in a daze, he urged the mare through the shallow stream. His brothers followed, their heads on a swivel, as they took in the area with admiring eyes and quick sweeps of their heads.

The four men wasted no time in felling trees to build a cabin. Teasing Thomas unmercifully about the number of young'uns he was bound to sire, being married to a woman as healthy looking as Lynn Celia, the four men laid out a cabin that was at least twice as big as was needed. Thomas took the badgering in stride. Smiling as he swung his broad axe, working the green logs into eight-inch square timbers that would form the walls of the cabin. Within four days they had completed the cabin, along with a snug privy set about twenty-five yards behind it. The cabin sat in the middle of the open area. Loopholes had been left between the logs so Thomas would have a clear view in any direction if trouble ever visited the meadow. While ranging through the woods in search of game, they had come on signs of small, scattered bands of Indians who had not yet acknowledged the treaty with South Carolina. Still, Thomas and his brothers worked on, hoping for the best.

The day after the cabin had been dried in, the four men combed the woods to the north of the meadow searching for rocks and stones suitable for a chimney. No more than fifty yards into the forest, they discovered an old, tumble-down cabin that had been used and abandoned by hunters sometime in the past. Its roof had consisted of nothing more than a network of interwoven saplings covered by a piece of sailcloth. The sailcloth was gone, removed by the hunters when they had walked away. Left to the elements, the cabin had quickly begun to decay. Thomas gave the door a slight shove; it broke loose from its rotted leather hinges and crashed onto the earthen floor within. Wary of snakes, he stepped through the opening and walked around the inside of the roofless structure, jabbing each timber with his hunting knife to test its strength. The bottom three layers crumbled under his touch; termites, along with the weather, had taken their toll, but the top five rows of well-cured white oak were still solid. He smiled as he resheathed his knife. Being able to use the good logs would allow him to get a small smokehouse up in no time.

The next morning, while Absalom and Matt continued to scour the area for building stones, Thomas and Luke began prying the walls of the old cabin apart. It took less than half a day to complete the destruction and haul the salvaged logs to the meadow.

Four days later, after the two men had lashed down the last row of cedar shakes on the roof of Thomas's new barn, they sat straddling the roof pole, admiring their work and drinking in the beauty of the sunlit meadow below them. Thomas waved towards the cabin where Absalom and Matt were busy setting stones for the chimney. Absalom paused in the midst of setting a stone and hallowed to them across the waving broom straw. By tomorrow, the firebox would be high enough that they could begin placing the stones closer together in order to narrow the chimney for the final few feet above the roofline.

In less than three weeks the four men were back in Augusta. There, they bragged to anyone who would listen about the beauty of Thomas's farm and the quality of the buildings they had erected on it.

* * * *

Leading a pair of horses burdened with their belongings, Thomas and his family set out two days after his return to Augusta. Lynn Celia and Patience took turns riding atop the pack of the more lightly burdened animal while Thomas led the way on foot. Thomas's old dog, Champ, trailed along at the rear, pausing every so often to sniff the air for food or enemies. The newlyweds laughed and gabbed like pilgrims going to the Promised Land as they plodded along to the northeast. They took their time, arriving at their new home late in the afternoon of the third day.

As they came out of the woods, Thomas halted at the stream, allowing Lynn Celia to take in the wonder of the spring and meadow for the first time.

"Oh, Thomas!" she gushed, tears welled up in the corners of her eyes. "It's even more beautiful than you described!" She shook her head in wonder. "There are no words to do it justice."

Thomas smiled and patted her thigh through the thin material of her skirt. This would be where their life together would take place; they could ask for nothing more. When Lynn Celia looked down at him, smiling her crooked smile, Thomas felt he had crossed into paradise.

"Come on," he said, still grinning. "I can't wait to carry you over the threshold of our own home." He turned and led the packhorse into the stream.

As he splashed through the shallow water, Patience shrieked a warning. It was only one word, but to a frontiersman, it spoke volumes.

"Indians!"

CHAPTER SIX

South Carolina Frontier
June 1, 1756

In one smooth motion, Thomas dropped the lead rope, cocked his musket, and spun about. He froze, hunched in a defensive crouch, weapon held at the ready. Lynn Celia instinctively reached out and hauled Patience onto the horse with her. She fought to hold the alarmed animal steady while clutching both children protectively to her breast. Champ produced a growl at the back of his throat; the hairs along his spine bristled as he confronted the intruder.

Leaving his pack animal in mid-stream, Thomas moved towards his family, planning to place himself between them and the danger. There was a single warrior standing beside a tree not fifteen yards behind them.

Damn! Thomas cursed himself. He must have passed within ten feet of the Indian without seeing a thing! Before he could move past her, Lynn Celia cried another warning and pointed in the direction of the meadow. Five more figures had popped out of the tall broom straw. They stood in a semicircle, silent and menacing. For one fleeting instant, Thomas thought of giving Lynn Celia's mount a slap on the rump in the hope the animal could sprint back to the main trail and escape before the Indians could react. With luck, they could make it to the settlement at Ninety-Six. He abandoned the thought as two more Indians stepped into view downstream.

Both of the newcomers were women, they looked as stunned as he did. Thomas eased the hammer of his musket forward into the notch of the doglock, placing it at half-cock. To show he held no hostile intentions, he cradled the weapon in his arm as he turned to face the five men in the meadow. With his heart hammering at the base of his throat like a frenzied blacksmith, he held up his hand as a sign of peace and waited to see what they would do.

They stood stock still, studying him. After one long minute, their leader forced himself to smile. It seemed to take an enormous amount of energy for him to force the ends of his lips upwards as if it was distasteful for him to display friendliness. He held the gesture for only a few seconds before it disappeared and his lips sank into a scowl. Without taking his eyes off Thomas, he slung his musket over one shoulder and grunted to the others. They all stooped and retrieved several tightly pressed packs of skins lying on the ground at their feet. The two women jumped the shallow waterway and scurried to the main group. They swung their own packs onto their backs. Without a sound, the entire group moved past Thomas and his family. Neither party spoke a word, but their eyes were clouded by the inherent distrust of each side for the other.

Thomas did not move until the Indians had stepped back onto the trail and padded off in the direction of Augusta. Once they were out of sight, he blew a long breath and sank to one knee, unmindful of the chilly water. "That was close." He shook his head in relief. "I thought our goose was cooked!"

"I can see now why that German fellow was so skittish about Indians," Lynn Celia said in a wavering voice. She was still in a mild state of shock at the suddenness with which the danger had appeared. "Were they Cherokees?"

Thomas shook his head. "Catabwas, I think. They were most likely just resting alongside the spring. They're usually friendlier than that. I think we startled them as much as they did us."

"I don't see how that could be possible!" Lynn Celia exclaimed. She burst out laughing now the danger was past, and allowed Patience to slide to the ground. The girl looked in the direction of the departed Indians. "Why didn't Champ warn us?" she asked; her small forehead wrinkled in worry.

"They had the wind on old Champ, it wasn't his fault," Thomas answered. He held out his hand to her. "Come on, little bit." He grabbed the child by one arm and swung her onto his shoulders, patting her knee affectionately. "Scared?" he asked, rolling his eyes upward. She nodded somberly.

He smiled up at her. "I don't blame you. Me, too." He turned his smile on Lynn Celia. "Just think of the story we'll tell our grandchildren about this one day. Threatened by Indians right here in our own meadow!" His eyes came alive as he surveyed the area, imagining what it would look like in thirty years. He had a great many plans for their future.

One job still left to Thomas was fashioning a mantelpiece for the hearth. Early the following morning, he shouldered his musket, grabbed his ax, and set out to find a likely tree of straight-grained black walnut. He followed the stream out of the meadow and into the woods to the west. Craning his head upward as he walked, he judged the suitability of each tree. He found one no more than a hundred yards from the cabin. Leaning his musket against a nearby tree, he draped his coat over the muzzle and rolled his shirtsleeves up past his elbows. He was just about to begin his first cut when a sudden voice arrested his movement.

"Howdy, neighbor." The voice came from behind him. Caught by surprise, Thomas spun around, holding the ax in both hands like a weapon. He found himself face to face with a tough, wiry-looking man about his own age. The man was cradling a long-barreled fowler in his arms. His smile seemed genuine as he dropped the butt of the musket to the ground and extended his right hand. His handshake was firm and strong; he seemed a straightforward man.

"Didn't mean to sneak up on you," the stranger apologized. "I was just lookin' to bring down a turkey 'round here. Name's Cub Hall, just moved in myself 'bout three months back." He jabbed his thumb over his shoulder, indicating the general area to the east. "I have a hundred acres of land 'bout a mile down the path there. Been seeing your smoke for the past few weeks, thought it was time to mosey on over and get acquainted."

The two men talked for over an hour before Cub left, promising to return with his wife that evening.

Just before sunset, Cub appeared in the Simpson's meadow with his wife, Eunice. Both of them sat astride a tall mule saddled only with a blanket. Thomas eyed the mule enviously; his two horses with their shaggy coats looked puny beside it.

Eunice, seventeen, was a light-complexioned blonde with a pale dusting of freckles across her nose and cheeks. She was as slightly built as Lynn Celia, and when the two of them stood side by side, they appeared to be cast from the same mold, then handed to different painters for finishing.

The Halls had only been married five months before they migrated from North Carolina. They had both been born and reared as Quakers, Cub explained, but couldn't abide being strangled by other folk's ideas. While Thomas and Cub talked farming, hunting, and politics, the two women sat by the fire gabbing like a pair of magpies. Across the room, Patience tended to Roger like a miniature mother, always hovering over him, ready to pluck the little fellow from any danger. Once the baby had found he could crawl, it had become a constant battle to keep him from tumbling into the spring or cooking fire.

Eunice had brought along a covered basket containing baked sweet potatoes and a roasted turkey wrapped in bacon slices. Cub had managed to down the bird on the way home after his meeting with Thomas. He proudly told the story.

"Flushed him from the brush beside the trading path and shot him on the fly," he bragged. "Prettiest shot you ever seen." He patted his long-barreled fowler affectionately. It lay canted against the front wall of the cabin.

The turkey and sweet potatoes went well with the crackling bread and tea Lynn Celia had fixed. She apologized, embarrassed at her meager contribution to the meal. Explaining that they hadn't time to plant a crop.

Thomas and Cub discussed their plans for the future. With a neighbor nearby to lend a hand, they would be able to get a sight more work done than they had originally counted on.

Cub had been raised with the belief that crops should go in the ground on the first day of April if they were to make any sizable harvest. Thomas agreed, lamenting that he was already two months late. Cub said he envied Thomas his natural meadow, pointing out that he could plow half of it without having to clear any trees while setting a cow to grazing on the other half.

"I don't mind tellin' you," he said to Thomas, "I wish that my place lay so good. I'd have me a fine farm in no time at all."

91

Loving Lynn Celia

Both Thomas and Lynn Celia swelled at the compliment, proud that their decision to swap land had found favor in the eyes of others.

"You don't know of anybody here 'bouts that has a fresh cow for sale, do you?" Thomas asked.

Cub shook his head. "Can't say as I do, but there ain't many folks about these parts. You could likely find one in Ninety-Six, though I fear the price they would ask for it. I could let you have a couple of piglets cheap; my sow just presented me with twelve new ones. All we'll have to do is catch 'em and notch their ears with your sign."

And so, Thomas became the proud owner of a future herd of hogs. As Cub pointed out, "He was lookin' at next year's ham and bacon on the hoof."

Thomas and Lynn Celia persuaded their guests to stay the night; they talked like long-lost friends, instead of people who had known each other for only a few short hours. Thomas told Cub he planned on making a trip to Ninety-Six for a cow and some chickens after he had his corn crop in. They talked it over and decided they would go together when the time came.

* * * *

Thomas spent the next day turning the rich, black earth of the meadow with his *Jump and Coulter* plow. The soil turned easily. As he followed the wooden blade through the deep furrows, a contentment he had never known settled within. *This was his land!* he thought to himself. The realization made him feel alive and indestructible.

He was halfway through the job when a hidden rock grabbed the plow, forcing his horse, Kate, to an abrupt halt. As the animal dug in and surged forward again, Thomas heard the unmistakable sound of snapping metal; his heart sank. Fearing the worst, he lay the plow on its side and inspected the damage. The coulter had been forged with a hidden flaw about three inches from the top, just where it would receive the brunt of the abuse. A bubble had formed inside the iron, forming a hollow and weakening it. It had only taken one sudden shock to snap the blade.

Dejectedly, Thomas removed the broken coulter and unhitched Kate. He led her to the barn and gave her a good rub down before heading, slumped-shouldered, to the cabin. Inside, he gruffly accepted a bowl of samp from Lynn Celia, who studied him with concern as he pushed his chair away from the puncheon table with his foot and plopped into it. Despite his somber mood, he ate greedily while she dug through the ashes of the fire, exposing a small covered pot containing four sweet potatoes. She forked one onto his plate without comment.

After finishing a quiet supper, Thomas sat outside in the fading light, resting his back against the logs of the cabin and taking steady pulls on his long clay pipe. He kept a close eye on Roger while Lynn Celia knelt at the edge of the stream, scrubbing plates and tankards with handfuls of white sand. They were both proud they had pewter plates to eat from rather than the plain wooden trenchers most frontier couples had to be contented with. Lynn Celia couldn't resist giving Thomas a worried look over her shoulder from time to time, knowing that some trouble had descended on them. She wondered what it was, knowing that Thomas would turn the question over and over in his mind until he had come up with a solution for the problem; then he would confide in her. Until then…

Patience, hovering over Lynn Celia with a candle lantern, cast her own questioning looks from one stepparent to the other. As she turned to look towards Thomas, she moved the lantern, Lynn Celia lost the light; she clicked softly with her tongue to regain the girl's attention. The light swung back into place.

"Sorry, mama," Patience said.

A warm feeling flooded Lynn Celia. She kept her head down as she scooped up a fresh handful of sand from the creek bed and scrubbed another plate. A happy tear coursed down one cheek and dropped into the stream where it merged with the current as it began its journey to the sea. It was the first time Patience had acknowledged her as such.

In addition to providing light, the candle attracted insects by the hundreds, much to the delight of Champ, who romped about the circle of light, dodging from side to side and leaping and spinning in a succession of futile attempts to snatch the buzzing insects from midair.

Lynn Celia and Patience gathered up the tankards and plates and headed back to the cabin. As she neared Thomas, their eyes locked for one brief instant, he smiled and blew her a kiss. She smiled in return, the problem, whatever it was, had been solved.

When she reemerged from the cabin, Thomas reached out and patted her on one hip. "I'll need to go to town tomorrow." He said. "The Coulter on the plow's broken. You reckon the two of you can make out by yourselves for one day? We'll be back by night."

Lynn Celia hesitated, the image of Indians sprouting from the meadow flashed across her mind. What would she do if they returned and Thomas was not here? She forced a smile and gave him a half-hearted nod, not trusting herself to speak; the fear would be all too evident in her voice.

Thomas studied her. "You sure?"

Her eyes swept the tree line on the far side of the creek while she mustered the courage to speak. She nodded, wiped her hands on the front of her apron, and turned away, ashen-faced. When she stepped back into the cabin, Thomas followed her inside.

She stood with her back to him, contemplating the flames in the hearth.

"I reckon I shouldn't have asked that of you," he apologized. "I wasn't thinkin'." He folded his arms around her and rested his chin on the crown of her head. "We'll all go."

Lynn Celia turned within the circle of his arms and pressed herself to him. "No, I've got to get used to being a frontier wife. It's just that those Indians the other day put such a fright into me!"

"I'll draw the load from the gun and put in fresh powder and buckshot. I'll leave it with you. Cub can take his musket."

Lynn Celia shook her head without looking up. "Won't do any good," she confided in him. "I've never shot a musket in my life."

Thomas pushed her away and held her at arm's length. He stared down into her upturned eyes. "I'll show you right now. There's nothing to it. You just wait until anybody stands in the doorway before you pull the trigger and you can't miss."

* * * *

Thomas led his mount down the muddy street of Ninety-Six. Cub sauntered along at his side, musket canted at an odd angle over one shoulder. They had walked the last mile to rest the animals before they were loaded for the return trip. Thomas could feel the small pouch suspended by a leather thong bumping against the center of his chest as he walked; it contained a good portion of the cash money he and Lynn Celia still possessed.

The small village contained a blacksmith shop, a flour mill, a trading post, and a tavern, along with a few cabins scattered throughout the local area.

Two of the cabins were new, their peeled logs still bright and oozing sap.

"Let's stop off at the smithy first," Cub suggested. "We may as well find a Coulter 'for we look for anything else."

The two men followed the ringing sound of the smith's hammer to a low building across from the trading post. They soon found themselves face to face with a burly man whose forehead was beaded with sweat despite the cool day. He wore a white work shirt, stained by soot, with the sleeves rolled up past his elbows. The skin of his lower forearms was pink and smooth as if hair feared to grow below his elbows. Everywhere else the man was covered in coarse black hair. When he looked up and spoke, his teeth seemed to appear and vanish within the curls of his thick beard.

"What can I do for you?" the smith asked. He continued pounding a short metal bar into shape as he waited for their reply.

"Lookin' for one of these," John said over the pealing of the hammer. He held out the broken Coulter for the smith's inspection. The hammer paused in mid-air.

"Ain't that something? I'm just putting the finishing touches to a new one right here. That is, if you're in the market for a new one. It'll save you a sight of money to fix the old one though; iron's mighty dear in these parts."

Thomas bobbed his head in agreement. He swallowed. "I've set my mind on a new one. What you reckon it'd cost me?"

The smith laid his hammer down and flipped a piece of ash from the corner of one eye. He rubbed his chin through his whiskers as he thought. "I'd say two, maybe three shillings." He shot Thomas a questioning look; one eyebrow was raised skeptically.

Thomas stood, dumbstruck. That was quite a sum, more than he had expected. Forcing his voice to sound calm, he asked, "What's fixin' the old Coulter worth?"

The smith grinned a smile that made Thomas feel he was not alone in his need for money. The gesture seemed to say everyone else in the area was in the same boat when it came to cash money.

"I could fix it for say ... one shilling. Cash on the barrel head."

That still seemed like a steep price to fix one strip of iron, but compared to the price of a new one... Thomas agreed. Thomas shook hands to seal the bargain, then headed for the trading post with Cub.

Loving Lynn Celia

The man inside introduced himself as Robert Gouedy. He explained he had opened the store as a trading post five years back. His main customers were Cherokees who preferred to save themselves a trip to Charleston with their skins. When he found that they had both recently moved into the area with their families, he slapped each of them on the back like long-lost brothers and offered them a drink of rum. "What can I do for you gents?" he asked after they had both drained their cups

Thomas's gaze ran along the shelves built into the back of the store. They were piled high with all types of goods. He saw a roll of bright blue cloth, the exact shade of Lynn Celia's eyes, and pointed it out.

Mr. Gouedy smiled. He circled behind the counter and took it down. "This catch your eye?" He lay it on the counter and unrolled it. "Not much left," he said. "The Indians are real partial to blue." He rubbed an edge of the material between his thumb and forefinger as he calculated its value. "There's just about enough left for one dress— that is if the woman ain't overlarge. If you want it, I'll let you have it cheap. Say three buckskins?"

"What's a buck goin' for now?" Thomas shot back.

Gouedy pulled a worn ledger from beneath the counter. "This is the latest schedule of prices," he said after removing a folded sheet of paper from it. He unfolded the paper and lay it flat on the counter, making sure Thomas could see it too. "Let's see..." his finger traced a line down the page before stopping suddenly. He looked up. "Twelve shillings." His tone indicated this was clearly a paltry sum for goods such as this.

"That's one and a half pounds for the cloth!" Cub whispered loud enough for Gouedy to hear him.

"That's right," the trader said with a smile. He thrust the roll of material towards Thomas. "That's because this is top quality; came straight from a mill in England. Here, feel it."

Thomas hesitated, his eyes traveled along the shelves, taking in all the other merchandise he could buy for that price. Still, his love for Lynn Celia urged him on. "Would you consider one pound? That's a powerful lot of money," he said. Leaning forward and placing his elbows on the counter, he continued in a conspiratorial tone, "I'm talkin' cash on the barrel head; white money. It'll save you trucking the skins all the way to Charleston to sell them."

A smile lit Gouedy's face at the mention of silver. "I'd say you've done some tradin' before young man!" He smiled and thrust his hand forward to seal the bargain. "Alright, it's a deal! What else do you need?"

CHAPTER SEVEN

Simpson's Meadow, South Carolina
June 6, 1756

Lynn Celia sat with her back against a stump at the edge of the meadow, her bare feet crossed before her as she worked on braiding a sheaf of plant fibers into a string. Patience stood behind her, watching over her shoulder. Nearby, Roger sat on his rump, his tiny hands clutching at Champ as the dog danced about him in teasing playfulness.

Eunice, who had walked over for a visit, knelt at Lynn Celia's side, demonstrating how to twist the plant fibers into a strong, flexible string they could use to bind bundles of broom straw together to make brooms.

The three of them had spent the morning working with Thomas's shovel inside the cabin, digging up the leftover roots and knots of grass still embedded in the floor. Now, as soon as they finished their broom making, they planned on sweeping it smooth.

As she tied the last knot, Lynn Celia held the broom up and swished it back and forth to make sure it would hold. It did. She stood up and brushed the dry residue from her apron.

"Your turn, Patience," she said in a voice filled with pride in her success. She lay the broom on the ground alongside the stump and stooped to bundle another batch of broom straw. Thomas's mare, Kate, grazing nearby, noticed her and ambled over, thinking the straw was all hers; she stopped and stood looking on in disappointment as the three humans ignored her and continued their work.

Patience giggled as she worked, reveling in the grown-up feeling of being included in *women's work*. Her small fingers were perfect for making string; in no time, she had a neat coil twisted and ready for use. Eunice complimented her as she completed the task. Her broom was almost as fine as the one Lynn Celia had made.

When they were finished, Lynn Celia sat on the ground, her legs crossed as the three of them giggled and chatted. She stopped in mid-sentence and stared when Eunice suddenly stood up and stretched, rubbing her lower back with a low moan.

"Why Eunice!" Lynn Celia exclaimed. "I believe you're with child."

Eunice smiled as she pulled the fabric of her dress tightly across her abdomen, displaying a slight bulge. "Does it show?" She asked, smiling with embarrassment.

Lynn Celia hopped to her feet and threw her arms around the other woman. "Why yes, it does! I'm so happy for you. Does Cub know?" Eunice blushed. "He ain't noticed it yet with these loose gowns. I've been waitin' on the right moment to spring it on him." "Oh! He'll be thrilled!" Lynn Celia said and rubbed the bulge gently.

"I know," Eunice agreed. "He's always talkin' about startin' a big family. I guess now it's begun." She rubbed her back again and, rolling her eyes, blew out a noisy breath. "My own ma had thirteen."

"Mine had only me," Lynn Celia lamented. "She took it cruel hard that Da had no sons." She let out a sad huff. "I just hope I don't take after her. It's been mighty hard for me to get one. It took three years before Roger was born."

"Give it time. You know what they say, a watched pot never boils."

Both women looked at Patience, who stood staring wide-eyed at Eunice as if expecting the baby's arrival at any moment. The two women burst out laughing.

"It won't come for a while yet," Lynn Celia explained. "From the looks of it, I'd guess, what? Six months?"

"I'm thinkin' five." Eunice corrected her.

"Even better!" Lynn Celia responded.

Gathering up their brooms, the trio began a slow walk back to the cabin. The two women walked in front while Patience tugged a resisting Roger along behind.

They were almost back to the cabin when movement caught Eunice's eye. "Injuns!" she cried. Grabbing Patience's hand, she hurried towards the door. Lynn Celia scooped up Roger and trotted at her side, clutching the child to her chest. Eunice slammed the door shut almost before the four of them crowded through it. Champ remained outside, roaming back and forth across the front of the cabin, growling and barking defiance at the intruders.

Handing Roger to Patience, Lynn Celia grabbed Thomas's musket from its pegs over the door. She pulled it to full cock.

"Ain't you gonna check to see it's loaded?" Eunice asked her, wide-eyed with concern.

"It is." Lynn Celia assured her. "I fired it this mornin', and Thomas put in a fresh load 'fore he left." She jerked her head in the direction of

Thomas's cartridge box hanging beside the door. "Be ready to hand me a paper cartridge if I have use for it."

She thought for a moment. "You ever loaded a musket before?"

Eunice grinned at her. "I was weaned on one."

The two women waited breathlessly, spying on the approaching party through the loopholes in the front wall.

"You watch out the back!" Lynn Celia snapped at Patience when the girl threw her arms around her waist and tried to burrow into her side. She returned her eye to the loophole; the same eight Catabwas they had seen when they arrived in the meadow a few days ago, emerged into full view. They headed straight for the spring. Lynn Celia noticed the one who had seemed to be the headman was limping. He had his right arm thrown around the shoulders of one of the women for support. There was a tourniquet tied just below the knee of his left leg. Even from across the meadow, both women could see him grimace as one of the warriors helped the woman lower him to the ground.

The Indians worked fast. Almost before the injured man was on the ground, a warrior produced a knife and began cutting on the leg. Seconds later, he bent over and applied his lips to the wound, then rose up and spit a stream of blood off to one side.

"Snake bit," Eunice said without taking her eyes off the scene. There was relief in her voice. "I thought for a minute we were gonna' have trouble with those red heathens."

Lynn Celia drew in and exhaled a relieved breath. She turned her face to Eunice.

"What should we do?"

"Stay put and see what happens. Pray our menfolk show up soon."

As they continued to watch, the other woman with the group disappeared into the forest. She returned in less than a minute with a handful of roots. She moved straight to the spring and washed them clean of dirt before popping them into her mouth. Her jaws worked fiercely as she chewed them into a pulp.

Having sucked the wound clean of venom, the warrior sat up on his knees and motioned to the woman. She spit the glob of root into her hand and rubbed it into the bite in a slow circular motion. Once she had it applied, she held it in place while the other woman wrapped a piece of linen several times around the wound. Very gently, she placed her hands on each of the man's shoulders and eased him onto a makeshift pillow. Once she had him settled, she spread a brightly colored Hudson's Bay blanket over him.

Lynn Celia's heart went out to the woman. She could make out the anguish on her face. She recognized it immediately as love. As she watched, she became aware of the fact that the woman had a dark reddish tint to her hair. She lowered the musket and leaned it beside the door.

"Have you noticed one of those women is white?" She asked Eunice. Eunice, keeping her eye on the loophole, nodded. "I saw her when they passed the cabin on the way to Augusta the other day. I don't think she's more'n half-white though. Probably the get of some Frenchman or trader."

For the first time since the excitement had begun, Lynn Celia turned her attention to Patience. The young girl was dutifully manning a rear loophole, her shoulders shaking with sobs. Lynn Celia moved to the girl's side and lay a reassuring hand on her shoulder. She leaned forward and whispered in her ear. "The bravest of people are those who can still do what needs doin' even when they're scared enough to cry." She gave Patience an approving smile. "I'm proud of you, daughter."

Patience rubbed her nose with the back of one hand and turned a tear-streaked face upward; she forced a grin. Lynn Celia gave her a slow kiss on the crown of her head and looked towards Eunice. "Keep a watch on them while I cook us something to eat." Lynn Celia knelt and stirred the coals, exposing the red-hot embers below to the air; within minutes, the fire blazed to life.

Eunice frowned at her, guessing her purpose. "You're thinkin' of takin' that out to them red savages," she said in a tone that clearly made it a statement, not a question.

"Doesn't the Good Book tell us to do so?"

Eunice shook her head. She turned her attention back to the loophole. "It also says to turn the other cheek. That don't work too well with Indians either. The menfolk'll be back 'fore dark," she said. "It would be best to wait 'til then. Safer too."

After stacking a dozen cakes of fried cornmeal onto a pewter plate, Lynn Celia opened the front door of the cabin and headed towards the meadow. Eunice slammed and bolted the door as soon as she was outside; seconds later the muzzle of the musket was thrust through the loophole.

Lynn Celia paused long enough to take a deep breath before continuing on. The small knot of Catabwas turned and watched her approach in silence, all except for the woman with the reddish tint to her hair. She continued to bathe the wounded man's forehead with a piece of wet osnaburg. Lynn

Celia knelt and placed the food beside the woman. She looked into her eyes; they were a pale shade of green. She spoke softly, trying to ask questions about her past, but the other woman simply stared back, not understanding a single word. Lynn Celia took a deep breath, rose to her feet, and made her way back to the cabin, forcing herself to walk despite the powerful urge to break into a run and hightail it back at top speed.

Eunice bolted the door behind her as soon as she entered. She shook her head and sank onto one of the puncheon benches alongside Lynn Celia's table. "Well, at least we know they don't plan any devilment," she said in a relieved voice. She shrugged her shoulders before adding, "At least for now."

* * * *

After saying goodbye to Cub at his cabin, Thomas continued on his way. He followed the Cherokee Path westward, turning off and heading through the thin layer of woods that separated it from Simpson's Meadow. He immediately spied a thin column of smoke alongside the spring, a lazy gray spiral curling upward into the evening sky.

He froze, his eyes sweeping the entire meadow. Feeling naked without a musket, he loosened his tomahawk in the waist of his breeches and moved ahead. From the corner of one eye, he kept track of every movement within the small knot of Indians camped alongside the spring.

Almost as soon as he stepped into the open, the door of the cabin swung open and Lynn Celia stepped out. Eunice followed, lugging his musket with her; she let the butt slip to the ground and seemed to sigh. Thomas noticed the musket was as tall as she was. Neither woman moved to meet him.

He tied Rodie to one of the porch posts and removed his dusty cocked-hat, holding it in his hand as he wiped the sweat from his brow with the back of one wrist. Without a word, he followed the two women inside. Eunice handed him the musket and bolted the door.

"How long they been out there?" he asked with a jerk of his head in the direction of the spring.

"About two hours. The older one is snake bit," Lynn Celia said. "I don't think they plan any devilment, but it would please me greatly to spend the night with Eunice and Cub."

Thomas scowled. "I'm not about to leave my own place just 'cause a snake bit Indian is layin' by the spring." He turned to Eunice. "As soon as I unload Rodie, you mount up and light out for home. Cub'll be worried sick if you're not back soon." He paused, then added, "The road's clear between here and your place."

"What should I tell Cub?"

"Just tell him to stay put. These Indians are just passin' through. But if he hears any shootin' between now and the time he sees those Indians pass by, tell him to high tail it to Ninety-Six and have Mr. Gouedy turn out the militia. We signed the muster roll this afternoon. There's about thirty of us." He paused and looked around the room. "Not that it'll do us much good."

After storing his packs inside, Thomas stood under the overhang of his small porch, musket cradled in his arm, as he watched Eunice guide Rodie through the trees and back onto the road, where she gave a quick wave and kicked the contrary animal into a canter. Rodie had expected a nice rest in his own barn. He was surly now that he was heading away from it.

One of the Catabwas, hunched over by the fire, watched her go, his head turning to follow her until she disappeared to the east. Thomas backed into the cabin and bolted the door. While he ate a quickly prepared supper, Lynn Celia told him the story of the Catabwa's arrival.

Thomas nodded when she finished. He swallowed a mouthful of food. "You did right givin' them the food. I don't know overmuch about these Catabwas, but I been around a heap of Creeks and such in Augusta; I can even speak Muscogee well enough to make a trade. They all expect hospitality. If you treat them right, they generally act pretty good."

He let out a quick, barking laugh and added, "Unless some fool gives 'em liquor!"

* * * *

The next morning, Thomas instructed his family to remain indoors with the musket loaded and at hand. He grabbed the repaired coulter and headed for the barn. Fifteen minutes later, he led Kate into the meadow where his plow, resting at the end of his last furrow, still lay canted to one side.

He inserted the coulter and resumed turning the soil, keeping a wary eye out for any movement from the Indian camp. Other than two of the younger warriors standing with folded arms by the spring, they seemed to take no notice of him.

That night Lynn Celia made another delivery to the Catabwas. The man with the snake bite was sitting up, alert. His leg was swollen and discolored, but he seemed to be recovering. He bobbed his head courteously as he reached for the plate and said a few words in his language. Although she didn't speak the language, she could guess the meaning by the tone of the man's voice and his facial expressions.

"You're welcome," she said, as he returned the plate from last night's visit.

The Catabwas remained by the spring for four days. That morning, the older man, along with the mixed-blood woman, appeared at the cabin. They paused about fifteen yards away and hailed loudly. When Thomas opened the door and stepped out into the early morning fog, he could barely see the dim forms of the other Catabwas breaking camp behind them. He waited for the two visitors to speak. The man limped forward and stopped at arm's length. He spoke a few words and thrust an elaborately carved soapstone pipe forward. Thomas took it, and the man stepped back. Thomas held the pipe out, appraising it in the dim light.

"Thank you," he said with a slight bob of his head.

The woman stepped forward. She looked down as she spoke. When she looked up, she made it plain through signs that she wanted to speak to the woman of the cabin.

Thomas called over his shoulder. Lynn Celia emerged and moved to his side. The woman smiled and held out a necklace consisting of shells and polished stones.

"Can you tell me your name?" Lynn Celia asked the woman as she took the gift.

"Maybe we can get word to your kin."

The woman smiled and bobbed her head in agreement to Lynn Celia's words, clearly unaware of their meaning. Without another word, the two Catabwas turned and padded off. As soon as they rejoined the rest of their party, they trekked away to the east. Patience came out and watched them depart, waving and shouting goodbye in childish innocence. The older woman waved back as she followed at the rear.

"It's a shame the woman couldn't understand us," Lynn Celia said. "I feel a sorrow for her family, not knowin' what's become of her."

Thomas threw his arm around her shoulders and drew her to him. "Most likely born to a Catabwa woman of a white father. He probably doesn't even know she exists. From the way she acted, she's never known anything else."

CHAPTER EIGHT

Simpson's Meadow, South Carolina
May 8, 1758

The cry of a newborn issued loud and lusty from the Simpson cabin.

Thomas, sitting outside on a puncheon chair, leapt to his feet. He paused and looked towards Cub, smiling proudly.

"It sounds like I'm a father again!" he exclaimed.

Since the birth of his son, Richard, last year, Thomas had looked forward to, as he and Lynn Celia put it, *havin' a houseful of young'uns*. He patted the back of his son as the one-year-old nuzzled against the base of his neck. His slumber disturbed by the excited movements of his father, the child scowled and ground his face into the cape of Thomas's hunting frock before releasing a slight sigh and dozing off again. Thomas smiled down at the straw colored hair and brushed his cheek across the wispy strands on top of the tiny head.

Roger, now over three years old, tottered around the clearing collecting sticks for kindling as Champ bounced around him in irregular circles.

The two of them could not be separated. When Roger clambered up into the loft each night, Champ would look up at him and howl like he had treed a coon until Thomas forced him outside to his assigned post and bolted the door.

At the sound of the first hearty cry, both boy and dog stopped and peered towards the cabin. Champ stood, poised like a pointer, his tail rigid and his nose aimed at the source of the sound. Roger dropped his small bundle of sticks and came bounding towards the cabin like a yearling deer, eager to know if he had another brother or a new sister. He had stated earlier that he needed a bigger brother than the one he already had, one who could run, jump, and play as intensely as himself.

Thomas turned to watch the door, expecting it to open at any minute. When it didn't, a gnawing dread began eating away at his insides. It was over an hour before the door of the cabin swung open and Prudence Usher, an experienced midwife whose family had recently settled in the area, stepped out into the gray overcast of a cloudy morning. It had been threatening to rain for the past several hours, but so far the sky had produced little more than a few oily gusts of sluggish wind. Thomas noticed Prudence had blood on her arms up to her elbows. The serious set to her face startled him, his mouth dropped slightly open. He felt his throat constrict.

"Something went wrong," he said, already knowing the answer. He turned and handed Richard to Cub, not trusting himself to hold the child any longer. The strength seemed to drain from his arms as he stood there; his face paled. "She's not..." He paused, not allowing himself to say the dreaded word, dead.

"I think you'd better saddle that mare of yours and ride to Ninety-Six for Doc Hatcher," Prudence managed to whisper as she exhaled an exhausted breath and sank onto the puncheon chair. She was a middle-aged woman of forty, but her face, drawn and tired from strain and worry, seemed much older. She studied her bare feet for a moment before her head jerked up. "No, she's not dead, but she's been bleedin' bad. I've tried everything I know to stop it..." Her voice trailed off as she threw her hands up in despair. She shook her head and grimaced. When she spoke, she didn't look up.

"Cub, you better ride for the doctor over to Ninety-Six and leave Thomas here."

Thomas looked towards Cub, who surrendered the baby to Prudence and trotted away to round up one of Thomas's horses. Thomas took a deep breath and stepped into the dim interior of the cabin.

The fire was the first thing he noticed. It had been banked against the rear of the hearth by an ashen-faced Patience, who at eleven years of age was very aware of the seriousness of the situation. Thomas held out his hand to her in greeting and they briefly touched fingertips before he pushed aside the patchwork quilt that had been rigged across the center of the cabin.

Lynn Celia lay on their bed, her face ashen, her features drawn. The newborn rested face down on her chest, whimpering and shaking its head as she caressed its back. A bucket of warm, reddish water Eunice had used to bathe the infant sat to one side.

Lynn Celia forced a smile as he entered. He took her by the hand and sank to one knee alongside the bed. They exchanged sad smiles.

"It's a girl," Lynn Celia announced proudly. "I plan on callin' her Egrain, after my mother."

Thomas nodded his head in agreement, only half-hearing the words. His mouth knotted in anguish as he fought to hold his emotions in check. Lynn Celia suddenly shivered, her whole body convulsed beneath the thin linen sheet that covered her.

"I'm so cold!" She managed to say through chattering teeth.

Thomas was instantly on his feet. After ripping down the quilt and throwing it over her, he ordered Patience to build the fire to a roar. He located every piece of covering in the cabin and piled it on his wife, then sat on the side of the bed and wrapped his arms around her. The movement woke the baby and it cried feebly as it searched for its first meal. Before Lynn Celia could react, Eunice plucked the child from her and cradled it to her own breast, bouncing it gently and cooing to it. She backed away and whispered to Patience, who raced out of the door.

"Where's Patience goin'?" Lynn Celia asked feebly as the patting of Patience's small, bare feet faded in the distance.

Eunice continued to pat and bounce the baby. "I've sent her to get Creasy up the road. We'll need her to nurse little Egrain along with her own child." When Lynn Celia started to protest, Eunice shushed her with a quick stare. "You can't chance drainin' your body anymore. Just sit back and rest. Egrain will be taken care of, you needn't worry on that count."

Thomas sat alongside the bed in a trance, stroking Lynn Celia's damp and disheveled hair

121

and studying her face as if he would never see it again.

* * * *

Cub urged his lathered mount forward. He had kept it at a steady canter for seven miles before allowing it to drop to a slow trot a mile short of Ninety-Six. People in the cabins along the trail stopped their chores and stared, open-mouthed, as he passed through the little village, knowing some great tragedy was being played out somewhere down the road.

He turned onto a narrow trace that led to the west, in the direction of Doc Hatcher's home, and allowed the animal to drop into a slow walk. Its flanks were flecked with lather and its head had begun to sink towards the ground. It was a plow horse, not used to such windy exertions. When the small cabin came into sight, he hallooed a dark-faced woman washing clothes in the front yard. The woman looked up and called back over one shoulder before going back to her work.

Cub lit alongside the hitching post and rested his hand on the tie rail as he waited for the doctor to appear.

Doc Hatcher was a tall, lanky man with arrow-straight black hair that hung limply on his head. He busied himself with pulling it back into a queue as he stepped through the door of the cabin. Outside, he stood in the sunlight, appraising his visitor.

"Who is it?" he asked, knowing only some dire emergency would drive a man to risk spoiling a horse. Without waiting for Cub's answer, he jerked his head in the direction of a small barn and bellowed across the sandy yard.

"Jenkins! Saddle up Sadie for me." He paused for just a moment, nodding to himself as he appraised Cub's mount. "Strip the saddle off of this one and put it on that white mare we've just broken." He cut his eyes in Cub's direction. "Hope you can ride a green horse, it's the only other one in the barn." When Cub said he could, Doc Hatcher invited him inside. "Might as well finish my tea, it'll be a bit before Jenkins gets done."

Inside the cabin, Cub explained the situation at Simpson's Meadow. Doc Hatcher nodded his head, injecting a few dilatory, *yes, I see's* as he gathered up his instruments and rummaged through a small chest while deciding on what other items should be stuffed into his saddle bags. When he was satisfied he had all that was needed, he slung the worn leather bag over one shoulder, signaled for Cub to follow, and marched outside like a preacher on the way to confront a backsliding sinner. Outside, he threw a long, stick-like leg over the saddle of his horse and surged off down the road without waiting for Cub.

Cub hopped onto the white mare. The animal, still not resigned to the saddle, gave a few unhappy kicks, spun in a circle, and brushed against a wall of the cabin in an attempt to dismount the rider from its back. When Cub proved to be too deft for such antics, the animal started forward at a lope, then dug in its front legs, sliding to an abrupt halt in a vain attempt to catapult Cub from its back. It started to run again, but Cub wrenched the reins savagely to one side, halting the animal in its tracks. "Give me a club!" he snapped at Jenkins, who was standing with folded arms, enjoying the spectacle. "I'm gonna need something to knock some sense into this damned animal!"

Jenkins produced a homemade riding crop from inside the barn. He handed it to Cub with a mischievous grin. "I forgot that," he said sheepishly.

The crop, made of a shaved hickory limb, was about three feet long and as big as a man's thumb. Cub swished it savagely alongside the animal's head a few times and kicked it in the ribs. When it hesitated, he gave it a solid *whack* on one flank. The horse jumped and grudgingly started forward. Cub grinned over his shoulder and nodded a farewell to Jenkins as he urged his cranky mount down the lane. Ahead of him, he caught a glimpse of Doc Hatcher as he disappeared around a small curve, already halfway to Ninety-Six.

When Doc Hatcher arrived at the Simpson's cabin, he was greeted like his arrival heralded the second coming and he was the Savior. In the eyes of Thomas, that is exactly what he was. In the last few hours, Lynn Celia had continued to slip away. Her bleeding had stopped briefly, then reappeared before slowing again after she insisted, *pigheadedly*, as Thomas put it, on nursing her own child.

When Doc Hatcher entered the cabin, he removed his hat and placed it on the table. Dropping his saddlebag alongside of it, he moved to Lynn Celia's bedside, where he stood surveying her and nodding his head in approval of the midwife's precautions. "Hips elevated, that's good," he said, looking towards Prudence Usher. "Did you pack her with clean cloths?"

"Yes sir, I did."

He gave the midwife another nod of approval. He reached out and rubbed the back of the infant's head. "It's a good thing you let her nurse," he said without looking up. "Many midwives wouldn't have done so in this situation, but I've always found a nursing mother stops bleeding quicker after the birth." He looked up into the guilty faces of Eunice and Prudence. "Oh, I see. Whose idea was it?"

"It was mine," Lynn Celia confessed. "I couldn't risk goin' on without at least caring for my own child."

Doc Hatcher smiled. "Just goes to show why God gave women their maternal instincts. Most of the time, everything works out for the best when they follow them." He straightened and shrugged, settling his coat more comfortably on his shoulders before looking at Eunice and Prudence.

"You two come here," he said. Pulling back the covers, he showed each of them where to place their hands, one on each side of Lynn Celia's abdomen.

"Push here. Keep the pressure on until I tell you different. If you get tired, sing out and someone will take your place. It's going to just be a matter of waiting now, you've done about all that can be done. Meanwhile," he fished in his saddlebag and pulled out a small glass vial. "I'll give her a taste of this. It'll help the blood clot." He looked towards Thomas. "You have any rum around here? I'll need it to cut this medicine. It's a mite vile tastin' and potent. The rum will help her get it down."

Cub appeared about thirty minutes after the doctor, his face was red with strain and fatigue when he came into the cabin. Flinging the hickory onto the table, he dropped onto one of the puncheon benches. "That was a mighty mean way to get your horse broken, Doc," he protested with a grimace. "If I'd had a gun, I would of just as soon shot the thing and walked home."

"She is still a might skittish. A man from up in Long Canes gave her to me to settle his bill. Said she'd be worth a pretty penny when she was broke."

Cub snorted. "Well, you might as well name her Penny, because she's damn well broke now!" He laughed and shook his finger in the doctor's direction. "Just remember if I ever need you, I have money on account for this. Lots of it."

Doc grinned. "I'll shake on it when we get the time." Setting his empty cup on the table, he stood and strode over to the bed where Eunice and Prudence were still keeping pressure on Lynn Celia's abdomen. He looked down at her face for a moment and laid his hand on her forehead. He looked satisfied when he turned away.

He stayed the night. In the morning, after Lynn Celia had recovered enough to eat a bowl of chicken broth, he pronounced her well enough that he could depart. Before he went, he sat with them and patiently explained it would be wise to settle for a small family. Lynn Celia was such a slight woman that it may be dangerous for her to try for a child every year as so many other wives did. Lynn Celia would not hear of it, she was adamant that she was as healthy as any other woman.

When the doctor said his goodbyes, he was certain they would ignore his advice. He need not have worried, try as they might, Lynn Celia would never conceive again.

G.G. Stokes, Jr.

CHAPTER NINE

Simpson's Meadow, South Carolina
November 1, 1759

Muster day. The birds chattered in the clear wash of sunshine. There wasn't a cloud in the sky. Thomas and Cub walked, side by side, at the head of the straggling column of eight men, neighbors who had moved into the district during the past three years. The foremost topic of conversation was the harvest the year had produced. Everyone agreed it was the best crop they had ever seen. They came at it from all angles, analyzing everything from the methods they had used in the planting to the timing of the harvest. To a group of farmers, this subject was much more relevant to their lives than the drilling they could expect when the militia gathered at Gouedy's Store.

There was trouble up north with the Cherokees, but it was far away and evoked little concern among the men as they strolled along the old Trading Path. The old trace was now a full-fledged road, with carts and wagons rumbling between Ninety-Six and Augusta on an almost weekly basis; sometimes old-style pack trains plodded by, their panniers stuffed with skins or trading goods.

The men were decked out in their Sunday best. The stocks around their necks were spotless and pressed, their coats were brushed clean, and any missing buttons had been returned to active duty. There wasn't a wife in the country who wanted her man to look like a ragamuffin on militia day. Why, the whole community would be watching them drill on the trampled grass beside the store!

The men were also caught up in the desire to represent their area well. They had spent yesterday cleaning their muskets. Many had sharpened or replaced dull flints before sanding the barrels until they shined like silver shillings. Stocks had been rubbed down with wax to hide the blemishes caused by years of heavy use. Thomas had even taken a whetstone to his old French bayonet, the only one the group possessed, and honed it to razor sharpness. It flapped in its scabbard against his thigh as he stepped along in the bright sunshine.

The small group paused at the woodline to survey the scene before Gouedy's Store. The area was crowded with more people than Thomas had seen since his last trip to Savannah. *There must be at least two hundred people here*, he thought, as he led his group forward. There were people of all ages, men, women, and children; white, black, and red. Several tents had been set up along one side of the narrow road. Shrill voices filled the air as their owners hawked goods carted all the way from Charleston.

The small knot of men stopped first at Gouedy's Store to sign the muster list before wandering around the crowded town. The militia would not drill until noon. That gave them an hour on their own. Several contests were in progress throughout the town. A competition among the owners of the new rifled guns caught their attention. Standing to one side, they watched the men place well-aimed shot after well-aimed shot into a circle no bigger than a man's hand at a distance of one hundred paces. To men used to hunting with smooth bore muskets, it was an amazing feat.

A tall, dark-complexioned man held out a finely crafted rifle for Thomas's inspection. "Care to try your luck with one of these?" He spoke with a heavy Pennsylvania Dutch accent.

"I make the best shootin' pieces you'll find anywhere on the frontier," the man said. "I apprenticed under a gunsmith up in Pennsylvania by the name of Martin Meylin before he died 'bout ten years ago. There got to be a right smart of gunsmiths up around the Lancaster area, so I

131

decided to try someplace where the competition wasn't so keen." As he spoke, he brushed an oiled rag across the lock and barrel of the rifle. "I served with the Virginia Regiment for a few years up in the Shenandoah Valley. Moved down here when the land opened up last year and took up a piece over to the east of here. It took a bit to get settled in, but now, I've got my shop set up and I aim on doin' some good business over the next few years. Go on, give her a try." He pushed the weapon in Thomas's direction. "All you need to do is prime the pan. I've already loaded her."

Thomas handed his musket to Cub and took the weapon. He dropped the butt to the ground and studied the muzzle. "That's a mighty small hole and a right thick barrel, ain't it?"

The man guffawed. "It ain't no musket. With this weapon you can put a ball anywhere you want to up to a hundred yards away. Even farther once you get used to it. Here." He dropped a small lead ball into the palm of Thomas's hand. "See how small the ball is? Forty-five caliber. Almost half the size of the musket balls you're using."

Thomas studied the ball. Rolling it in the palm of his hand, he looked towards Cub who said, "Don't look big enough to stop anything, does it?"

The man chuckled. He pointed to an old iron frying pan hung from the limb of an oak tree fifty yards away. "Take a bead on that 'fore you say anything," he said.

Thomas flipped the frizzen of the rifle forward and primed the pan. He closed it with a sharp metallic snap and knelt, laying the weapon across the top rail of a fence that zigzagged along the edge of the field. Noticing the rear sight for the first time, he looked up at the gunsmith with a silent, questioning look. The man knelt alongside him. Using his fingers, he explained how to use the rear sight, something not found on a musket. When Thomas nodded, he gave him a pat on the shoulder and stepped back, out of the way of the touchhole which would send a horizontal jet of flame out as the weapon was fired.

Thomas took in a deep breath, exhaled half of it, held the tip of the front sight on the center of his target, aligned the rear sight, and squeezed the trigger. Across the field, the iron pan pinged and spun in a fretful circle as the ball spattered on it. With a smile, Thomas looked up. The German smiled back. "Load her up," he said. "Try it again, so you'll know it wasn't just luck."

Thomas reloaded, shaking his head at the tightness of the patched ball as he rammed it down the barrel. Two more shots produced identical hits. The other militiamen were astonished.

Thomas shook his head in wonder. "What you askin' for her?" His voice was hesitant, dreading the price which was sure to be high. The Dutchman held out his hand. "First off, my name is Christopher Christ. See, that's my mark right there on the lock, C. Christ. He was one of those people with an almost too firm handshake. "I sell these plain lookin' rifled guns for twenty pounds. The fancy ones with all the brass and silver inlays can go as high as fifty." He watched Thomas's face as he named his price, gauging his reaction. As expected, he saw shock and disappointment at the price. He smiled. "Sounds high to you?" When Thomas simply whistled, he motioned for him to follow him to his cart. From beneath a canvas tarp he pulled out another rifled gun. "This one I can let go for ten pounds. It's used and it's plain, not even a butt plate, but it is just as accurate as the fancy ones with their patchboxes and nose caps."

Thomas studied the weapon, turning it over in his hands as he weighed the cost against his family's welfare. He and Lynn Celia had ten pounds tucked away. This would take it all. It was a hard decision, he desperately wanted the rifle. Still, he couldn't bring himself to spend the last of his cash money. He shook his head and handed the rifle back. "It's a fair price, I've no doubt about that, but it would wipe me out. I'm sorry, but no."

Christopher shook his head. "I wish I could go lower, but ten pounds is as low as I can go without givin' it away." He tucked the rifle back beneath the tarp. "Remember me when you're able. I'll have some more made by then."

From the porch of Gouedy's Store, a voice bellowed for the militiamen to fall in for muster. The voice had an urgency to it that caused the men to hurry as they formed into their companies. An officer, dressed in a red coat with green facings, paced the porch impatiently. He wore a sword; the tip of the scabbard thumped each time it crossed one of the floorboards. When the lieutenants had their men drawn up into some semblance of a formation, the officer turned, stood stiffly erect, and eyed them with a sour expression. He took a deep breath before he began.

"My name is Captain Jeffery Jameson, of South Carolina's Independent Company of Foot. I have been sent by Governor Lyttleton to ready a regiment of militia that will stand by here, at Ninety-Six, until he arrives to take command. We are marching north, to Fort Prince George with the intention of chastising those Cherokees who have been committing depredations along the border as far north as Virginia. The governor is convinced they intend some sort of mischief in this colony also, and he is determined to thwart them at the earliest possible moment. Therefore, half of you will be required to reassemble here in three days and join with the men from other militia regiments who are moving to this site even as we speak. Bring a weapon and ammunition, a canteen, a bedroll, and enough food for a week, as well as any other equipment you think will be necessary. Let me caution you to travel light, we will be moving at a rapid pace once we march." He cleared his throat and seemed to search for something more to say. Then contented himself with, "Your officers will select those men who are to march. That is all."

The assembled militia fell apart, buzzing like an agitated beehive. Thomas, in shock, looked at the other seven men.

"Who's to go?" he said the words more to himself than to the others. He looked at

Cub. "One of us should stay here. I'll volunteer to go if you'll look after my folks while I'm gone." He looked at the other men. "Y'all may want to do the same thing. We don't want to chance having any of our womenfolk being left alone at a time like this. Find someone you trust to watch 'em and follow me to see the Lieutenant."

In the end, Cub volunteered to go with Thomas and two of Prudence Usher's unmarried sons, James and Hezekiah.

"I can't let you go by yourself," Cub said, shaking his head when Thomas objected. "It just don't seem right. We'll get some of the new men in the area to look in on the womenfolk while we're gone."

The four men walked to the store where a harried clerk checked off their names on the muster roll. "You will each be issued powder and lead as needed. Bring your own bullet mold," he said with barely a glance in their direction. Waving them aside, he motioned for another group of men to step forward.

Loving Lynn Celia

CHAPTER TEN

Fort Prince George, South Carolina
December 26, 1759

Governor Lyttleton was proud of himself. He had just diverted an Indian war, of that he was certain. These Cherokees, he thought to himself, were mere children, devoid of the slightest ability in anything requiring higher-order thinking. One had only to take a firm hand with them to control them.

As a result of the treaty, twenty-four Cherokee men, including several headmen, had been given up as hostages to ensure the conditions of the agreement were met. They had been marched off immediately and imprisoned in a small log structure that had originally housed six noncommissioned officers of the garrison. The remainder of the Cherokees had departed in a surly mood.

Thomas, feeling relieved, watched them go. He, and the other militiamen, had trekked northward, thinking they would be invading a hornet's nest of bloodthirsty savages. Instead, their life had been fairly mundane, no fighting had occurred and not a man had been lost.

That evening, the four men from Simpson's Meadow sat around their fire, chatting of home as they devoured a meal of fish pulled from the nearby Savannah River. Thomas tossed the bones of a native trout into the fire where the four men watched in silence as the small ribs blackened and curled in on themselves before being devoured by the flames.

"Ain't you gonna eat, Kiah?" James Usher asked his brother. Hezekiah ran his hand across his forehead and shut his eyes. He shook his head. "Don't feel much like it tonight, James. I've got some sores in my mouth that sting something awful when I chew." He ran his tongue around the inside of his cheek and grimaced at the tenderness. He had been suffering from a fever and aches for over a week. Several other militiamen had been complaining of the same ailment.

"Take a good swig of this." Cub offered Hezekiah his canteen. "It's good English rum I got off'n one of them soldiers at the fort. Hold it in your mouth for a while before you swallow.

Kiah took a long pull and handed the canteen back to Cub, who offered it to the other men. They both yawned and shook their heads in refusal. Cub shrugged his shoulders and jammed the cork back onto the spout. Infected by the gaping yawns of the others, he lay back in his blankets and dozed off.

* * * *

"Oh, my Lord!" James's outcry jolted Thomas awake. He sat up in his blankets and reached for his musket. Across from him, Hezekiah lay on his side, propped up on one elbow. He spit a thick, bloody glob on the ground. When he turned his face towards Thomas, it was flushed, and his neck was speckled with the unmistakable rash that precedes smallpox. Thomas's first impulse was to jump to his feet and move away as quickly as possible. Instead, he remained transfixed, stunned at having come face to face with death. He glanced towards Cub and James; both of them looked on the verge of panic.

Thomas cleared his throat as he tried to think. "Either of you had the smallpox before?" he asked. They both shook their heads, no.

"Me neither."

Hezekiah lowered himself back to the ground. He pulled the blanket up to his chin as a mighty shiver racked his body from head to toe. When it subsided, he moaned through chattering teeth, "You boy's best stand clear."

James cast Thomas a look of pure dread. "You two go find the surgeon," he said in a whisper. "I'll stay here with Kiah 'til you get back."

As they walked through the camp, Thomas and Cub noticed small knots of alarmed men. Four other cases had appeared during the night. Some of the militiamen were shoving their meager belongings into packs and preparing to move to safer areas, others milled about, hesitant to desert their sick comrades, but gripped by an overwhelming fear of the disease. At the fort's gate, they were halted by a pair of wary and hostile sentries dressed in the blue coats and black leather caps of South Carolina's Provincial Regiment. The sentries cautioned them to come no closer. It was obvious the news of the outbreak had spread this far - if not the disease itself. Turned away, they headed back to their fire.

Thomas stopped in mid-stride and snapped his fingers. "Why don't we find a man who has already had the pox and pay him to nurse Kiah?" he said.

The two men spent the next hour attempting to cajole or pay any man who displayed the unmistakable scars of the pox to nurse their friend back to health. In the end, they agreed the four of them would each pay two pounds to a short, weasel-faced individual who demanded half of the money in advance.

The man, Martin Grubb, accompanied them to their fire, rubbing his hands together as he anticipated the reward he had extorted from the desperate men. Thomas and Cub had assured him they could scrape together the money from their meager belongings. Thomas dragged his heels as he walked, a sudden feeling of exhaustion seemed to creep through his arms and legs. His back ached something terrible and he felt the first flush of a fever. The next morning, he too, was in the deadly grip of the smallpox epidemic.

The following week passed in a blur for Thomas. In rare and lucid moments, he caught short snippets of conversation from the men about him. Once, he looked up to see the white canvas of a tent overhead. As if in a dream, he heard the voice of Martin Grubb say the words, "He's dead," before drifting back into delirium. He was conscious, sometimes, of the overwhelming urge to claw at his body. It seemed to itch or burn over every square inch. It would have been unbearable torture were it not for his long periods of unconsciousness.

A week later, Martin Grub, who despite his disreputable appearance, had turned out to be the most conscientious nurse in the makeshift field hospital, knelt at Thomas's side and felt the pustules on his face and chest. "I think he'll make it, doctor," he said over his shoulder. "Run your fingers over these pustules."

A middle-aged man, who Thomas recognized as the post surgeon, knelt alongside the stretcher. There were no beds available, a pair of saplings with a canvas stretched between them was the best the sufferers could hope for in this wooded wilderness. The doctor probed the welts with his fingertips as Martin described what he was feeling. "Feels like he's been hit with a load of shot caught under the skin, don't it?" Martin said knowingly. "They're starting to scab over, which means he's through the worst of it. In another four or five days he can start to work on getting' his strength back. 'Course he won't never be as pretty as he was 'fore the pox got aholt of him"

With a tired grunt, the doctor rose to his feet. His knees popped as he straightened and his face had a pale green tint to it. "Mr. Grubb, you're mighty knowin' about this disease. I can't overestimate your value to the garrison and myself. Without you, we would have lost more men than we did."

"Why, thank you, sir," Martin said. He smiled at the unaccustomed praise.

Two mornings later, Thomas was moved to another area on the far side of the fort where those who were recovering and in the final stages of the disease were housed. Many others went straight from their makeshift beds to the fort's rude cemetery. The following day, he was allowed to walk along the river where other survivors strolled as they regained lost strength. He studied every face in an attempt to locate old friends, but the horribly scarred faces were sometimes unrecognizable until the scabs had all fallen away and the healing had begun. After looking into a borrowed mirror, he understood that the disease had not been kind to him. His face was pitted on the cheeks and forehead, and his neck was deeply scarred, as were his underarms. He plunged into a fit of depression, wondering what kind of reception he would receive back in Simpson's Meadow. In his mind's eye, he could see his wife and children recoiling in horror when they first saw him.

Cub came to see him the next afternoon with news that both of the Usher boys had died. For some reason, Cub had remained untouched by the disease.

"It's a sad thing for those boy's folks," Cub mused as he sat alongside Thomas. The two men took turns throwing sticks into the river, watching as the current whisked them away. "Neither of them had yet turned twenty." Cub shook his head and choked back a sob. "Half of us already dead and we ain't even seen a battle." His voice was both sad and angry.

Thomas looked up, suddenly realizing the area seemed deserted compared to what it had been before he had contracted smallpox. "Where is everybody?" he asked.

Cub snorted. "The militia near mutinied when the smallpox broke out." He tossed another stick into the current. "The governor marched them back home before they all deserted. Left us here to recover or die. The son-of-a-bitch!"

CHAPTER ELEVEN

Simpson's Meadow, South Carolina
Jan 21, 1760

Worry gnawed at Thomas's insides like a ravenous wolf as he neared his home. His steps were slow and hesitant as he led Rodie along the well-beaten trail. In his heart, he had never been secure in the thought that Lynn Celia loved him. After all, hadn't she married him simply to make a home for Patience? How would he be welcomed now, with his pale and pitted face? He let his imagination run wild, envisioning all manner of homecomings, most of them horrid.

Cub had dropped out of the little group of returning militiamen when they passed his cabin. Martin Grubb strolled at Thomas's side, whistling a tune as he swaggered along. His musket lay across his right shoulder, canted at such a sharp angle that the barrel protruded two feet to his left. As usual, it was primed and loaded. He, at least, had no reservations about where he was going; a new phase in his life was about to begin.

It was dark when Thomas halted in the trail to eye his cabin. A few pinpricks of candlelight escaped through the chinking between the logs. He made a mental note to plug them the first thing in the morning. He studied the clearing and barn for several long minutes, looking for changes, and telling himself he was searching for the things that needed to be done. But deep down, inside, he knew he was looking for a reason to postpone his return for a little while longer. His heart pounded in his chest and the palms of his hands were sweaty. He wiped them on the back of his trousers before rubbing his chin through the stiff whiskers of his beard. With the pitting on his face, he found shaving too much of a chore. Besides, he could never quite get the beard off, anyway. So, he had ignored custom and let his beard grow, although he did keep it closely trimmed. It had grown to be a comfort and hid the worst of his scars.

Beside him, Martin grounded his musket and rested his forearms across the muzzle. "This it?" he asked. "It's a right smart lookin' place."

Thomas nodded. "Yes, it is. I can't imagine any better place to call home." He took a deep breath to steady his nerves and held it for a moment. "Let's go," he said without taking his eyes off of the cabin.

Champ began barking as soon as they broke the cover of the trees. His challenges intensified as they drew nearer. Once the dog caught Thomas's scent, it bounded through the dry broom straw of the clearing, stopping to do a circular dance of welcome in front of its returning master. When Thomas knelt and rubbed the old dog behind the ears, Champ plopped his behind onto the ground and sat looking up in wide-eyed wonder. His tail beat a solid tattoo against the ground.

The door inched open suspiciously, then was flung back on its hinges when Thomas called out. Patience and Richard bounded from the door, calling his name. He remained kneeling, spreading his arms wide and letting his musket drop to the ground. He wrapped his arms around both children as they, in turn, threw their arms around his neck. He tousled his son's hair. "My, you've grown!" he said with a smile. Richard looked up to study his father's face. Slowly, the corners of his lips curled upward. He reached up, pulling inquisitively at Thomas's beard to see if it would come off. When it didn't, he tugged harder.

Swinging Richard onto his shoulders, Thomas marched towards the cabin. Patience walked at his side carrying his musket, and Martin followed a few steps to the rear. He gave a slight nod of hello to Lynn Celia, who stood transfixed in the doorway. A demure Egrain, thumb thrust into her mouth, stood at her mother's side, holding onto her skirt for support. When she recognized Thomas, she took a step forward and extended both arms upward, demanding to be picked up. Thomas scooped her into one arm, the other he held out to his wife.

Thomas's heart sank when he imagined a slight hesitation before Lynn Celia welcomed him with a kiss. She broke away and nuzzled her head against his neck, weeping quietly.

"I hope this face ain't scarin' you." Thomas spoke to the top of her head. Lynn Celia shook her head vehemently without looking up as she collapsed against him, her entire body wracked by uncontrollable sobs.

"I feared … I would never see you again!" she managed to gasp through her tears. "All those soldiers comin' through here with their stories about men dying like flies up there. How they were just thrown on the ground to get well or die, with no one to tend to them! I can't tell you how many times I started out to find you. If it hadn't been for the little ones… Oh, Thomas!"

Thomas's arm gripped her tightly as he felt her knees start to buckle.

"We best get on inside," he said, fighting to hold back tears of his own. "I don't know how long I can stand here holdin' up the whole family. By the way…" He motioned with his head in the direction of Martin who stood quietly to one side. "This is Martin Grubb. I owe him my life. Without his nursing, I wouldn't of made it through."

Lynn Celia stepped back and wiped her eyes with the hem of her apron. She gave Martin a nod. "I can't thank you enough Mr. Grubb. Please, come in. Anything we have is yours."

As they stepped inside, Richard caught the log above the door and lifted himself from his father's shoulders. He swung back and forth in the opening, laughing gleefully before dropping to the floor and bounding past the others like a scampering squirrel racing to nab the year's final chestnut. Thomas sat Egrain on the table and dropped onto one of the side benches with an exhausted sigh.

"You're still weak," Lynn Celia observed. "You shouldn't overtax yourself so." She sent Patience outside to stable the horses, shooed Richard and Egrain to the far side of the table, and took a pair of pewter plates from a stack on the mantle. "Mr. Grubb, if you'll just sit down right here, I'll spoon you two up what's left of the stew. I'm sorry there's not more left, but I wasn't expecting visitors." To Richard she said, "Climb up to the loft and fetch me down one of those hams hangin' from the ridge pole. These men are going to need a sight more food than what I've got cooked." When the men objected to her putting herself out for them, she shushed them sternly and set about preparing their meal.

"Where're you from, Mr. Grubb?" Lynn Celia asked over her shoulder as she spooned venison, stewed with wild onions and potatoes, onto the plates.

"Call me Martin, ma'am," he answered. "I'm from Virginia. I served with the Virginia Regiment under Colonel Washington until my time expired a year ago. I made my way down through North Carolina to Charleston. When the governor called out the militia, I marched along with 'em. That's how I came to be at Fort Prince George."

"Is that the same Colonel Washington who was with General Braddock?" she asked as she set the plates in front of the men and took a seat alongside her husband. "I read an account of him in a newspaper once."

"Yes'am. That's the one. I served under him for three years. I would calculate I rode a thousand miles chasin' Injuns up and down the Shenandoah Valley."

"Ever catch any?" Richard asked. He was sitting in the loft with his feet dangling in the air, looking down at the two men from above.

"Not often," Martin admitted. "Once or twice in the whole three years." "Did you kill any?" Richard's eyes lit up. This was interesting stuff to him.

"A few. They're mighty slippery." Returning his attention to his plate, he dipped a cold biscuit into the gravy and took a bite. "Mmm…" he moaned. "After what we've been eatin', this surely does hit the spot. Thank you, ma'am."

"You're quite welcome. Anything else you want, just ask." Lynn Celia gave Thomas an affectionate shake and kissed him on the cheek. "Nothing's too good for the man who saved my husband's life."

Loving Lynn Celia

CHAPTER TWELVE

Simpson's Meadow, South Carolina
January 25, 1760

Martin had disappeared every morning for the past three days on a secret mission. Following breakfast, he would gather up a sack of tools and troop off into the forest to the south. For the first two days, he had carried a mattock and shovel. Yesterday, he had swapped those tools for an ax and tomahawk. Each evening he returned sweaty and dirty, stopping at the spring to wash for supper. After eating, he retired to the loft of the barn where he had fashioned a comfortable bed for himself. He wasn't a tight-lipped man, but his daily doings were a well-kept secret. When asked, he refused to tell, saying, "I'll show you when it's done."

Thomas, who had come to consider Martin a bit strange as he came to know him, shrugged his shoulders and went about his own business. He had too much work to do to concern himself with Martin's arbitrary moods.

On the fourth morning, Martin announced he had something to show Lynn Celia and the children. He looked at Thomas and said, "You come along, too."

Loving Lynn Celia

Lynn Celia, leading Richard by the hand, followed Martin past the spring and across the meadow. Patience and Thomas followed behind, a chattering Egrain riding high on his shoulders. At Martin's request, Champ had been tied and left behind; howling in mournful protest, he watched them go. Both men had brought along their muskets. Martin stepped into the stream. He motioned for the others to do likewise. Once they all had their feet wet, he led them downstream, picking his way along the streambed to avoid leaving any traces of their passing on the sandy banks. A quarter of a mile downstream, he paused beside a large boulder that diverted the water to one side. A large oak, growing on the other side, had been partially uprooted by some long-forgotten storm. It leaned away from the stream at a sharp angle. A fork near the top held the trunk about five feet off of the ground. Its limbs were winter bare.

A flat area in the stone, near the base of the rock, provided a foothold that Martin used to scramble out of the water and onto the top of the boulder. Once on top, he reached down and helped the others to climb up onto a level with him. When they were all crowded together on top of the rock, he handed Lynn Celia his musket and pointed to the oak.

"Mrs. Simpson," he said, "y'all stay put right here and watch me real careful." With that, he stepped onto the tree and made his way along its horizontal trunk. Using his outstretched arm to help him keep his balance, he stepped gingerly along the top side of the trunk for at least thirty feet. He stopped and pointed to one of the branches with his finger.

"If you ever come this way at night, count the branches. This is the tenth one." Without waiting for a reply, he grabbed the branch and lowered himself to the ground. He knelt below the tree and brushed away a thin covering of dried leaves. Carefully lifting two clapboards he lay them aside to expose a small hole dug into the red clay. Grabbing the limb, he suspended himself over the center of the hole and dropped in. When he touched bottom, only his head and the tops of his shoulders were visible. "This is what we called a *hidey-hole* up in the Shenandoah," he called to Lynn Celia. "If the Injuns ever give you any trouble, you grab the young'uns and head here. Once you drop down and pull these boards over you, you'll be invisible except to someone who steps on the boards." He made a gesture with his hands to indicate the maze of limbs and branches around him. "That ain't likely. In the summertime, when the leaves sprout back out, a man could stand on the trunk right above you without seein' a thing."

Martin threw up his hand when Lynn Celia started to step out onto the tree.

"Hold on ma'am," he cautioned her. "The fewer people to cross here the better. The last thing we want is to beat down a trail that some sharp-eyed buck might spot."

Using the limb to pull himself out of the hole, he covered it over and swung himself up onto the tree's trunk. He looked towards Thomas. "Make sure y'all practice finding this hole so's you can make your way to it even in the dark." He continued to give instructions as he stepped back along the tree trunk. "And always stay in the water commin' down, so you won't leave no tracks." He paused halfway back, balancing himself on the top of the tree trunk. "I've dug it out in the bottom like a cache the trappers use for their pelts, it'll hold the whole family if needs be."

Lynn Celia stepped back as he clambered onto the top of the rock with them. "Do all of the people up there in Virginia have a *hidey-hole*?"

Martin was silent for a moment. He nodded. "Those that lived."

158

He studied her reaction for a moment. "With all the bad news we've been hearin' about those damned Cherokees, we best be prepared. You can't never tell when they'll start stirrin' up mischief around here." He looked towards Thomas. "You best get your missus a musket of her own. She won't be safe without one if we get called away to the militia again." He rolled his eyes in thought. "A rifle might be better. With a rifle you could keep a party of Indians pinned back in the woods all day. They'd not chance coming into the open against something like that." He shrugged. "In the dark though, better head for the hidey-hole."

* * * *

Before the sun had broken the horizon, Martin took up his musket and strolled away in the direction of Ninety-Six. He returned after dark. Pausing just inside the doorway of the cabin to eye its occupants, he dipped his head to Lynn Celia who sat off to one side with little Egrain in her lap. She was examining a spool of thread Patience had just turned out on the family spinning wheel. Thomas sat by the fireplace in his prized rocker, whittling dowels out of short pieces of hickory. Richard sat at his feet, feeding the wood shavings into the fire. Martin held his musket in one hand, in the other he held a new forty-five caliber rifle.

"What you got there?" Thomas asked. He made a motion with his head to indicate the gun. Martin held the weapon out, eyeing it as if he had just become aware of it. "Oh, this? It's just something I picked up over to Christopher Christ's this afternoon." Thomas recognized it as the rifle Christopher had tried to sell to him a few months ago.

"Times being what they are," Martin said. "I thought a rifle might come in handy." He pushed the door shut with his foot and set the weapon against the wall. Pulling a bullet mold from his hunting pouch, he lay it on the mantle alongside Lynn Celia's pewter plates. "I don't have room for all this in the barn, mind if I leave it here for safe keepin'?" He smiled owlishly. "Mind if I sit?" He plopped onto one of the benches alongside the table and looked around the room with a lazy expression. "Got anything to eat?"

* * * *

Martin spent the following morning teaching Lynn Celia how to load and fire the rifle. Thomas stood to one side with an amused expression on his face, watching as she fired a slow succession of futile shots at a pine cone Martin had set up as a target twenty-five yards away. All of her shots went wild.

Exasperated, Martin took the rifle from her and shouldered it himself, demonstrating the proper technique of sighting as he reiterated the proper way to aim and fire for accuracy.

"First, make sure the stock's seated tight against your shoulder," he said. "Take a deep breath, let half of it out, sight on the target, and squeeze the trigger. If you do it right, it should come as a surprise to you when it goes off." He dropped the weapon to his side and looked at her. "You're jerkin' the trigger," he scolded. "And closin' your eyes don't help none, neither." An idea formed in his mind. "I'll tell you what. We'll leave it empty and just prime the pan. That way you can practice your trigger pull without wastin' too much powder and lead."

For the next hour, Martin worked with his pupil. When Lynn Celia scored her first hit, he declared the lesson over.

"Thomas's musket seems so much easier," Lynn Celia said as she handed the weapon over to him. She looked up, batting her eyes innocently. "Wouldn't that be better than a rifle?"

161

His shoulders slumped. "If it's loaded with buckshot," he said in a flat voice. He looked towards Thomas, his dream of making her into a marksman shattered in an instant. "Is that ole' doglock of yours loaded with shot?"

Thomas nodded and smiled sheepishly. "It's double-shotted."

Lynn Celia looked at the two men. "What's that?" she asked.

While Patience went to fetch the musket, Martin set up a score of pine cone targets. Some he grouped together, others he scattered about at different intervals on the ground. He pointed to the main cluster. "Put your front sight on that group there. Remember, there's no rear sight on a musket. It don't need one anyways. Hold steady as you can and give the trigger a good tug, just like your husband showed you before." He grinned at Thomas.

When Patience returned, Thomas checked the priming in the pan and handed the weapon to his wife.

"It's a mite heavy compared to the rifle," she remarked as she held it to her shoulder. The muzzle rotated in a slow circle as she fought to keep it pointed at the pine cones.

"Go on," Thomas prompted. "Just pull the trigger when the front sight falls on the target."

With a solid boom the musket discharged. Lynn Celia went one way, the shot went the other. The cluster of pine cones exploded, scattering in all directions. Thomas reached out and caught his wife under her arms as she dropped the musket and tumbled backwards. Both men erupted into hysterical laughter.

Red-faced and scowling, Lynn Celia rubbed her shoulder and shrugged Thomas's hands away. She spun to face both men who continued to laugh at their idea of a joke. She gave Thomas an angry slap on his shoulder and stepped back to glare at her tormentors, she was not amused.

Patience began to giggle. It was infectious, spreading to Richard and finally to Lynn Celia. She shook her head and walked over to where the pine cones had been stacked. Studying the carnage for a moment she turned back to face the two men. "I think the musket works best," she said with a sly smile.

Loving Lynn Celia

CHAPTER THIRTEEN

Simpson's Meadow, South Carolina
February 2, 1760

Thomas halted Kate in the middle of the field, halfway through a new row. He let the plow fall onto its side and stood in the furrow as he scanned the woods to the east. He was sure he had heard a shout. He glanced at his musket that lay canted against a split rail fence separating his field from the pasture. He heard the voice again, closer now, but still too far away to be understood. Yet something about the tone of the voice made him move towards his weapon. He waved and called a warning across the field to Lynn Celia, who was sweating over an iron wash pot set amid a low fire. She stopped stirring and set her paddle aside. Behind her, Patience was beating the excess water from a freshly boiled shirt with her own flat paddle. When they looked his way, he motioned them towards the cabin. Lynn Celia scooped Egrain into her arms, she didn't need to be told twice. They had been hearing rumors of Cherokee war parties swooping down on the settlers up north. It was only a matter of time before they made their way this far to the south.

Unhitching his mare, Thomas threw his leg over her back and trotted towards the road. Whoever was yelling was coming along the trail from Ninety-Six. He recognized the first rider as Martin, cantering along the trail with Cub's oldest child riding behind. He was followed by Cub and Eunice, riding double on their tall mule. Eunice held her youngest child in one arm, the other arm she kept wrapped around her husband's waist with a deathly grip. As they drew closer, Thomas heard Martin's words clearly.

"Indians!"

"Where? When?" Thomas questioned Martin as soon as he drew to a halt. The dry dust kicked up from the trail swirled around them as they spoke. Thomas waved it away with his hand.

Martin set Cub's oldest boy on the ground and spit a piece of grit from his mouth. "Over to Long Cane. Three riders came into Ninety-Six about an hour and a half ago. They say that they was jumped by over a hundred mounted warriors yesterday." He shrugged. "Maybe two hundred. They managed to get away, but the last they saw of 'em, the Injuns was heading towards the settlement." He made an impatient gesture to the west. "I've got to go warn the other families. We'll set out as soon as we get enough of the militia together. Make sure the women are safe, then ride to Gouedy's. I'll be no more than an hour behind you." He spit again. "Make sure Lynn Celia has my musket; I'll take the rifle with me." Wide-eyed with excitement, he kicked his mount into a trot and rode away.

* * * *

Thomas halted Rodie at the edge of a small clearing. While scanning the area ahead for danger, he patted the shaggy, winter growth on the animal's neck. The horse threw up its head and snorted. Thomas leaned forward. "Smell something, ole' boy?"

To his left, another horse whinnied a greeting to an unseen visitor. Without a word, the party of militiamen slid from their saddles and took up positions behind the nearest trees. Thomas checked the priming of his musket and pulled the hammer back, releasing the doglock and bringing it to full cock.

Tense minutes passed. Many of their mounts snorted or whinnied. There were other riders nearby, of that they were certain. And those unknown men were keeping well-hidden on the far side of the clearing.

Christopher Christ, the gunsmith from Pennsylvania who had been elected captain after disclosing he had served as a sergeant in the Virginia Regiment, leaned forward from behind the cover of a downed tree and imitated the raucous call of a crow through his cupped hands. Silence. He waited, his head moving back and forth like a hound on a scent before motioning for Thomas and Martin to mount up and follow him across the clearing. He pointed to Cub and Wiley Jenkins, Doc Hatcher's indentured man, and, using hand signals, indicated they should circle to the right and left of the clearing, flanking anyone hiding on the far side. "The rest of you boys keep your eyes peeled," he whispered.

The three mounted men crossed the open area at a slow walk, their muskets held at the ready. Halfway to the far woodline they halted to appraise the danger. Other than the sound of a soft wind, all was quiet. "Let's move on," Christopher whispered. "Slow and easy. Be ready for anything."

Without warning, two horsemen plunged through the undergrowth ahead of them. They were Cherokees who had been spooked by the approach of Cub, who was threading his way through the trees to their right.

Without thinking, Thomas threw his musket to his shoulder, sighted down the long barrel, and fired. The trailing man threw up his hands and rolled, head over heels, off the back of his mount. To Thomas's right, the rifles of Christopher and Martin cracked and the second rider tumbled to the ground.

"Gee … Haw!" Martin whooped. He kicked his mount into a canter and raced across the clearing. Thomas and Christopher followed, but cautiously. By the time they caught up with Martin, he had already removed the scalp of one of the Cherokees and was strolling casually towards the other. The man was still alive, although badly wounded. He moved slightly. It was a feeble attempt to push himself upward onto his elbows. Thomas noticed that blood welled upward in little red geysers from the two bullet holes in his back as he struggled to rise. Martin placed his foot between the man's shoulder blades and pushed him brutally to the ground. He grasped the warrior's scalplock and pulled his head back to expose the unprotected neck to his knife, slashing the jugular with a quick twist of his wrist. He kept the head pulled back until the blood ceased to spurt, just the way he would bleed a hog. He removed the scalp with a liquid plop!

Martin, still kneeling beside the slaughtered Indian, looked up. "You want your'n?" he asked, shaking the scalp in Thomas's direction.

Thomas shook his head. He had lived his whole life on the frontier, had seen many a scalp in his day. But until now, he had never witnessed the actual killing and taking of one of the grisly trophies. It no longer seemed heroic. For the first time, he became aware of something dark and menacing in Martin. The man clearly despised Indians.

Christopher leaned forward in his saddle and spit a greasy stream of tobacco juice onto the dead man's back in a contemptuous gesture. "Mount up, Martin," he growled. "We got other fish to fry."

Cub, who sat his mount to one side, gave Thomas an uneasy glance. Thomas shrugged and looked away.

* * * *

The small party of militiamen approached the Long Cane settlement slowly and cautiously. The smell of wet ashes and charred timbers hung heavy in the air. A sickly sweet smell of decaying flesh was evident whenever the wind shifted and blew from the west. They clustered together as they rode, dreading what they would find.

After making a quick sweep through the settlement, it was clear it had been deserted before it was burned. A handful of abandoned chickens, pecking at the bloated remains of a milk cow, were the only living creatures in the area. Christopher waved the militiamen onward. They headed south, following the trail of the refugees.

"Looks like they lit out just ahead of that war party," Martin said. He had dismounted to study the signs in the trail a few miles below the abandoned settlement. He looked up at Christopher. "I'd say they didn't make it, sergeant. There's no way they could've outrun all them Injuns with their women and children taggin' along in wagons."

Christopher chewed on his lower lip as he thought. He came to some inner conclusion and shook his head. "Martin, you and Cub ride on ahead. Warn us if you spot anything. The rest of us'll follow about a quarter mile behind. No sense in riskin' an ambush."

Martin accepted the dangerous assignment without comment. Cub looked dubiously at their impromptu leader, but remained silent.

Thomas and the rest of the patrol watched the two men canter ahead, most secretly relieved at not having been chosen to accompany them.

The militia turned south, moving rapidly and relying on the scouts out front to warn them of danger. "Martin's the best damned woodsman I've ever met," Christopher assured Thomas as the two of them rode, side by side, along the narrow trail. "We served together for a while in the Virginia regiment under Colonel Washington. He can out Injun an Injun."

* * * *

An hour before sundown, they caught up with Martin and Cub, who were sitting their mounts alongside the trail. Martin threw up his hand in recognition as they came into sight. Christopher halted alongside the two men. They conferred in hushed tones, Martin gesturing towards the south as he spoke. When they finished talking, Christopher motioned for the other men to dismount and gather around him.

"There's a large party of men, settin' up camp ahead. From the amount of smoke, Martin thinks it's white men, but he ain't sure. Could be another party of militia. Could be a pack of savages." He waited for a response from the men. When no one spoke up, he outlined his plan. He would ride ahead with Martin to check on the camp. The rest of them would set up an ambush along the trail. If the enemy proved hostile, he and Martin would pick off a couple with their rifles and head back up the trail. When the enemy followed, they would ride straight into an ambush. Christopher looked at the circle of faces. He asked a few questions to make sure each man understood the plan. "Everybody remember the clearing we kilt them two Injuns in this mornin'?" The men nodded. "Good. If we bite off more'n we can chew, scatter and meet up back there." Christopher had been fighting Indians for years, he seldom left anything to chance.

The men waited for over an hour before Christopher and Martin came trotting back up the trail. They reined in and motioned for the men to mount up. "It's a bunch of Georgia militia from the other side of the river," he said with a grin. "They've been roundin' up survivors." He paused to spit. "The goddamn Injuns caught them folks from Long Cane a little ways below here and cut them to pieces two days ago. Killed over fifty people, we think." He made a careless motion with his hand to indicate the surrounding wilderness.

"They say there's women and kids scattered all over these woods."

That night they bivouacked with the Georgians who had already buried eighteen bodies. Several children, some of them scalped but still alive, had also been brought in. They were lying in the bed of a partially burned wagon. To Thomas, their moans sounded like the mewing of a litter of kittens. He glimpsed Doc Hatcher from time to time, moving among them, binding poultices over the ugly wounds. One child, no more than five years old, sat on the box seat of his parent's wagon calling plaintively throughout the night for his mother. She had not yet been found. Thomas began to understand the hatred Christopher and Martin held against the Indians. They had both seen such as this before.

The wagons stood where they had bogged down. Most of them had been burned. A few, for one odd reason or another, had escaped harm.

The survivors said at least a hundred mounted Cherokees had swooped down on them as the men struggled to free the wagons from a particularly nasty stretch of trail. Many of the men had left their weapons in their own wagons in order to keep their hands free as they worked. It was a fatal mistake.

With no means of defense, they had been easy prey to the attacking warriors.

The battle, such as it was, lasted less than thirty minutes before the surviving settlers took to their heels. There had been about a hundred and fifty of them, no more than seventy had been found.

The following morning, Thomas and Cub paired up with one of the survivors and searched the woods to the east. Around noon, they stumbled across the mutilated bodies of five people, two men and three women. They lay together in a heap where they had died, slowly and horribly. Seventeen-year-old Andrew Pickens, who had escaped the massacre and returned with the militia, identified them as the Norris family. The three men wrapped them in blankets and tied them across their horses. When they returned to camp, the four were buried together in a single grave. The militiamen set up crude markers so their families could find the site when they returned to visit the grave.

Early the next morning, despondent at not having found all the missing people, but apprehensive about the safety of their own families, the two parties parted and headed for home.

Loving Lynn Celia

CHAPTER FOURTEEN

Simpson's Meadow, South Carolina
February 6, 1760

Martin's hand shot straight into the air. He reined in his mount and turned sideways in the road, halting Thomas and Cub who were riding behind him. His face was invisible in the cloudy gloom of a quarter moon. "Something's wrong," he said as he upended his rifle on one thigh. "Cub, you stay here with the animals. Thomas and me will go have a look-see." They dismounted and handed their reins to Cub.

Before turning to follow Martin, Thomas flipped the frizzen of his musket forward and felt the priming with his thumb. Satisfied, he eased it quietly back over the pan. The two men moved forward like silent wraiths, the sandy soil of the roadbed muffling their steps. Martin knelt at the edge of the meadow and peered at Thomas's cabin from behind a tree. He leaned towards Thomas, who knelt beside him, and said in little more than a whisper, "Somethin' don't look right. No smoke commin' from the cabin. It's too dark to see clear, but it looks like the door's open too." He placed a

177

hand on Thomas's shoulder to keep him from leaping to his feet and moving forward. "Stay here and cover me. I'll mosey around to the other side of the clearing. When you hear three hoots from a crusty ole' owl, it's safe to come on in." Martin stood and moved in the direction of the road until he was certain Cub could see him. He motioned for the other man to lead the animals off the road and into the trees. Thomas's gaze followed him as he moved back into the bushes. When he blinked, Martin was gone.

Thomas could hear faint stirrings to his rear as Cub felt around in the darkness for branches stout enough to tie the animals to. A few moments later, Cub moved forward and knelt at his side. Neither man spoke, their total attention was focused on the cabin. What had happened? Where were their families? In the blackness, Thomas's imagination began to run wild.

A half hour dragged by before they heard Martin's signal. Still cautious, they led their mounts past the spring and to the cabin. They tied the animals out front. Inside, they could hear the rasping sound of flint and steel, followed by a dim glow as Martin succeeded in igniting a piece of spunk. Thomas's breath caught in his throat as the flame flared to life. The door of the cabin had been knocked off its upper hinge; it lay canted to one side of the narrow opening. He had to turn sideways and step over it to enter. Martin held the candle high to illuminate the interior of the cabin. Everything was in disarray; furniture was smashed or overturned, the mattresses were ripped to shreds, and everything of value seemed to have vanished from the mantle and shelves. Even the spinning wheel was missing. Fighting to keep a sudden rush of wild emotions in check, Thomas climbed into the loft. It was empty. Down below, Martin jerked the candle in his hand downward, extinguishing the flame and leaving them in utter darkness.

"Quiet!" he hissed when Cub mumbled something unintelligible. In the darkness, Thomas looked down from the loft and saw Martin's inky outline step to one side of the doorway. The clouds had cleared for a moment and a pale shaft of moonlight fell through the opening. Martin stood there, rifle held at the ready, sniffing the air like a lonely old hound. He stepped back into the gloom of the cabin and spoke over his shoulder in low tones.

"They've come back. Listen," he paused. Thomas could see the outline of the frontiersman's head rotating back and forth like a hunter following the sound of his prey. Thomas eased from the loft to the floor, leaned near the other man, and said in an almost inaudible whisper, "What is it?"

Martin answered back in the same low voice, "Nothin', that's the trouble. No crickets or frogs. No night critters of any type. Any other night they'd be raisin' a ruckus 'round here. Someone's out there, moving around, keepin' 'em quiet." Martin grabbed Cub's shoulder in the darkness and steered him towards the door. "Cub, you keep an eye out that door," he said, before gesturing towards Thomas, "You take the back window.

Keep off to one side, out of sight."

"What about our folks?" Cub demanded too loudly for comfort.

"I don't know," Martin answered. His voice had an edge to it that had not been there a moment before. "But I do know if you run off half-cocked and get yourself killed, it won't help them one bit."

In the darkness, Thomas could almost feel Cub deflate. Knowing just how he felt, he turned his back on the two men and peered through the smashed shutters of the rear window. He sensed a dark shape move alongside his barn and shook his head to make sure, but it was gone. *My eyes must be playing tricks on me,* he thought to himself. Behind him, he could hear Martin climbing into the loft. A moment later he heard the soft, brushing sound of sand raining onto the floor as the other man dug the chinking out from between two logs to make a loophole.

Thomas shook his head again. This time he had definitely seen a slight flicker of light between the logs of the barn. He hissed upward to get Martin's attention.

"I seen it," the other man called down quietly. A moment later his rifle cracked. "They're settin' fire to the barn," Martin said in a matter-of-fact tone. Thomas could hear him reloading as he spoke. "They must be young bucks out on their own. They ain't thinkin'. Once they get a fire goin', this whole clearin's gonna be lit up. There's no way in hell they can sneak up on us without losing some men. They don't like to risk a life if they don't have to." He paused, a moment later his rifle cracked again. Thomas saw a dark silhouette to one side of the barn drop to the ground. In less than a heartbeat the man was back on his feet and holding one arm pinned against his side as he disappeared around the far corner of the burning barn.

Up in the loft, Martin cursed, "Damn!"

The dry logs of the barn caught easily; within minutes, it was transformed into a raging inferno that sent fiery fingers of flame hundreds of feet into

181

the air. In the red glow of the firelight, Thomas could see that what he had thought was a small clump of broom straw, was, instead, Champ. The faithful dog lay on his side, halfway between the cabin and the barn, pin cushioned with arrows.

"Anybody see anything?" Martin called to them. The need for silence was long passed. When no one answered, he hung his head over the edge of the loft. "Cub, you better lead them animals into the cabin if you can. Those heathens may get the idea of leavin' us afoot."

"What about them Indians out there?" Cub called over his shoulder.

Martin gave his rifle a solid slap on the stock. "They know we got a rifle in here and someone who knows how to use it. They won't dare get close enough with those arrows and muskets while this light holds.

Outside a musket boomed. A few seconds later a spent ball bounced across the ground at the rear of the cabin and struck the bottom log with a solid thump.

"See," Martin said, vindicated.

* * * *

The night passed slowly. Twice, Martin sniped at dark outlines sidling from tree to tree, he was certain that he had wounded another one of their attackers. By mid-morning, without having seen anything for over two hours, Thomas felt he could wait no longer, he had to find his family.

When Cub insisted also, Martin sighed and shook his head. "Have it your way," he said. "I say give it a little longer, but..." He waved a hand in the direction of the door.

"Let's go. Mount up and stay spread out."

The three men fanned out across the clearing. Thomas discovered the missing spinning wheel beside the spring; several of its spokes had been broken and the ground around it looked disturbed. A scuffle had taken place there. He sat and stared at the ominous signs for a moment before he forced himself to look away. He shook his head to clear it. It could prove fatal to ignore one's surroundings at a time like this.

Cub was leading his mule around the far side of the clearing, looking for the slightest sign of his family. His movements were slow, lethargic, like those of a man who had gone too long without sleep. Martin had ridden into the woods to the north. Thirty minutes later he emerged from the east. He trotted his mount over to where Thomas sat astride Rodie. "There was five of 'em," he said, waving a fresh scalp in Thomas's direction. "Looks like one of them I winged last night, died. I found where they'd hid his carcass before they lit out." He cleared his throat. "They took your other horse. I saw her tracks on the other side of the barn."

The two men watched Cub as he zigzagged across the meadow. His eyes were down, searching the ground for any clue that would lead him to Eunice. "What'd you find?" Thomas asked as soon as he came up to them.

"They took at least one of the women with 'em," Martin said. "I saw her tracks over there to the north. Can't tell which one though."

"Goddamn it!" Cub snapped. "If we hadn't waited so long to do something, we might have saved her." His mule shied at the sudden outburst. He reached out and patted it on the neck to calm it as he glared at Martin.

"Could've gotten ourselves killed, and her too," Martin answered. "I've done this a hundred times. Have you? You push an Indian too hard and he'll split a captive's skull rather than let you get her back." He stared straight at Cub, then shifted his eyes to Thomas. When neither spoke, he said, "The more important thing is this. Where are all those that they didn't take?" He looked towards the stream. His meaning was clear. "Let's go."

The three men walked their mounts down the middle of the stream, heading for the hidey-hole. In the back of their minds was the same nagging question: *who was taken?* Thomas, his stomach churning, feared the worst. He halted his mount alongside the rock and stepped from the saddle onto its smooth top. Calling his wife's name softly, he treaded along the tree's trunk. Sweat trickled down his forehead and stung his eyes as he grasped his way from limb to limb.

Cub, not knowing where the hole was, circled the tree on his mount, calling Eunice's name into the twisted branches. Martin stood erect on the boulder, his rifle cradled in one arm as he surveyed the surrounding trees for signs of an enemy.

When Thomas was directly over the hole, he dropped onto the ground beside it. His throat tightened as he lifted the boards and tossed them aside. Emotion twisted his features. He saw a pale face, squinting upward into the bright sunlight, it was Eunice. As her eyes adjusted to the glare of the morning sun, she recognized him. A smile crept to her lips. She sighed in relief. "Thank you, God!" she exclaimed. As if the sound of her own voice had released the pent-up emotions she had kept bottled up inside during her ordeal, she began to cry. Tears cut bright furrows along her dusty cheeks as she handed the smaller children to Thomas.

Once the children were all safely deposited above ground, Eunice stood and thrust her head and shoulders into the cool morning air. Thomas reached down and helped her from the hole. He swung her to one side and reached down as Patience's head emerged from the murky dungeon. She looked up with red-rimmed eyes. "Where's Mama?" she gasped, as he pulled her from the hole.

* * * *

Back at the cabin, the women told their story. They had been warned of the raid by the sounds of musket shots coming from the direction of the Usher's cabin, a mile to the west. Did the men know anything about the Usher family? They wanted to know.

Patience sobbed as she told Thomas what had happened. Hearing the shooting, the women had bundled up a few meager belongings and hustled the children towards the safety of the woods. They were splashing down the stream when Patience had stopped and turned back towards the meadow. At first, she had stood like a statue, torn between the safety of the hidey-hole and the desire to return for her dead mother's spinning wheel. In the end, she couldn't bring herself to leave it behind. It was the only thing of her mother's she had left. She broke down completely, blubbering her story through a torrent of tears as she told how she had wrestled with Lynn Celia while the other woman had pulled her towards safety. She could still remember Lynn Celia looking over her shoulders in dread as they hurried along.

Patience had pleaded with Lynn Celia to let her return for that one remaining treasure as the small knot of refugees had made their way down the creek. They were almost to the hidey-hole when Lynn Celia had relented. Pushing Patience ahead of her, she had ordered her to lead Eunice and the children to the safety of the hidey-hole. She told them she would be back within half an hour. That was the last they had seen of her.

Patience gulped and wiped her cheeks with the hem of her soiled apron. "I'm so sorry! It's all my fault." She hid her face in her hands, heartbroken and guilty. "I feel so cowardly not chasing after her! But I couldn't leave Eunice and the children.

They would have never found Martin's hidey-hole without me."

Thomas eyed the sobbing girl, his lower lip quivering as he fought to hold back his own tears. He took a step towards Patience, who recoiled slightly, thinking he was on the verge of striking her. Seeing her fright, he spun on his heels and stalked away. Halfway across the meadow he dropped to his knees, beating the ground with his fists before rubbing the fingertips of one hand over his forehead. Like a man possessed, he jumped to his feet and marched to his horse. He swung his leg over the saddle.

Martin stood in front of Thomas's horse, looking up at him with his hands on his hips. When he spoke, his voice was stern. "Just where in the hell do you think you're goin'?"

When Thomas tried to steer his mount around the other man, Martin grabbed the animal's bridle.

"Let go of my horse, Martin!" Thomas growled. He gave the reins a jerk. The animal backed away, trying to pull free of Martin's grip.

"You damned fool! You're goin' to get yourself killed, runnin' off half-cocked like this. Where's your food? How much powder and lead do you have? What if they'll trade for her, what could you offer?" He paused and eyed the younger man disdainfully.

"Haven't give it any thought, have you?"

"Every moment we stand here gabbin', they're getting' farther away." Thomas said. He made an impatient gesture with one hand, indicating the area to the north of the meadow. "What would you do, let 'em have her?"

"I would get down off that animal and get some supplies together, that's what I'd do. Then, I would head after 'em, slow and easy. You think they don't know someone will be followin' them? You'd ride into an ambush 'fore you made it five miles."

Thomas frowned, rolling his lower lip inward as he thought. "All right," he said, sliding to the ground. "Let's get our truck together, before they get too far ahead."

* * * *

With their animals packed and ready, Thomas swung back into the saddle.

"Forgot anything?" Martin said, inclining his head in the direction of the children. Thomas slid to the ground and scooped Roger and Richard into his arms. He gave each of them a kiss and set them back on the ground. After kissing Egrain goodbye, and entrusting her to Eunice, he walked to Patience's side. He stood, looking down at the distraught girl. His thoughts raced. Dropping to one knee, he wrapped an arm around her and lay his cheek on the crown of her head. "You did right, not leavin' them," he said. "Without you to lead them to the hole, all of them would have perished." He gave her a reassuring squeeze. "We'll find Lynn Celia. Cub will see the three of you to my folks in Augusta." He raised his eyes towards Cub.

Cub nodded.

CHAPTER FIFTEEN

Fort Prince George, South Carolina
February 14, 1760

Leading their spent horses, Thomas and Martin trekked towards the gate of Fort Prince George. They had followed the trail of the Cherokees who had abducted Lynn Celia for four long days. The raiders had proved to be wily opponents. They snaked their way northward, doubling back on their trail at a different time every day to check for signs of pursuit. It was a very effective strategy. Yesterday evening, only Martin's keen senses had saved them from stumbling into an ambush that would have proved fatal. This morning, they lost the trail twenty miles south of Fort Prince George. Playing on a hunch, Martin had guessed the Cherokees would head for Keowee with their captive. If so, these were very bold Cherokees. The town sat within a musket shot of the fort.

As the two men came within sight of the fort, trudging along on foot and leading their jaded animals, a dispatch rider forced them to the side of the narrow trail. The wheezing, lathered animal was faltering, but the rider continued to urge it on with sharp raps of his riding crop. As the messenger disappeared behind the walls of the fort, the two men gave each other an uneasy look. Off in the direction of Keowee, a tight knot of Cherokees stood on the far bank of the Savannah River. They watched the two white men sullenly as they passed by.

Within a few minutes of the rider's arrival, a cannon boomed. Thomas watched as a gray puff of smoke dissipated over the southeastern bastion of Fort Prince George. Moments later a second cannon was touched off, both men increased their pace, knowing it was the signal for the garrison to rush to arms.

"Now what do you make of that?" Martin thought aloud. He turned to look over his shoulder at the Cherokees on the hillside. "Looks like they've had a few more join them," he said dolefully.

The fort was filled with the hubbub of excited voices as the two men stepped through the front gate. The sentries ignored them, their attention focused on the inside of the fort where the commander, Lieutenant Richard Coytmore, was conferring with the other officers of the garrison. One of the officers motioned to a sergeant who trotted over to them. The sergeant's head bobbed as the officer talked. He saluted, about-faced, and marched away shouting for the company to fall in. A corporal of the South Carolina Provincials pointed to the two guards and cursed them soundly for neglecting their duty.

Noticing Thomas and Martin standing to one side, he glared at them maliciously. Placing his hands on his hips, he drew himself up to his full height, which was significant, and demanded, "Who the devil are you two?"

"We've just arrived from Ninety-six," Thomas answered.

The corporal studied his face for a moment. He nodded and gave the two men a thin smile. "You've had the smallpox. That's good," he said, inclining his head in Thomas's direction. He looked towards Martin. "What about you?"

"I served as a nurse in the fort hospital back when Governor Lyttleton was here," Martin answered. "I never caught it." He motioned towards the milling mass of humanity inside the fort. "What's all the fuss about?"

The corporal pointed to the parade ground where the men were forming into companies. "Fall in over there an' you'll find out quick enough," he said. He waved them towards the milling throng.

Martin balked. "But our time in the militia is up, we—"

The corporal cut him off with an impatient gesture. "Tell it to the officers. Now, get! Fall in with the rest of the militia."

Dragging their feet, the reluctant recruits made their way across the dusty parade ground, heading towards a small group of nondescript frontiersmen who eyed them suspiciously.

"Who be you?" asked a tall, lanky fellow dressed in a blue canvas hunting frock.

Martin jerked his thumb over his shoulder, indicating the shouting corporal. "That noisy fella told us to fall in with the rest of the militia. That you?"

"Like as not. Who you with?"

"Ninety-six militia. Marched up here with Captain McIntosh 'bout three months ago. We're on the way north lookin' for this man's wife. She was taken by the Cherokees 'bout a week ago."

"You look plum tuckered out," the man said. His accent identified him as a frontiersman from some remote region. He gestured towards Thomas. "This scar-faced fellow looks like he's about played out, too."

Thomas scowled. He had no wish to be reminded of his disfigurement. He snapped a few angry words at the stranger, telling him so.

One of the other men gave Thomas a lazy smile. "Don't mind him none, he don't mean nothin'. Do you Winslow?"

Winslow eyed Thomas, sizing him up. "I reckon not," he mumbled sullenly.

The second man smiled. He thrust out his hand. "I'm Thomas Sanders, the sergeant over these fellas. Y'all fall on in, we'll get acquainted later."

With much cursing and cajoling, the sergeants herded their men into formation, where they stood silently while Lieutenant Coytmore, the fort's commander, addressed them.

His voice was deep and clear, easily heard and understood.

"Men," he began. "I have just received word that the Cherokees have attacked and killed fourteen men, not ten miles from here. Some of our people may have escaped. If so, they're scattered throughout the forest. I am sending out the militia to bury the dead and search for any survivors. The regular troops are to stay in the fort and ready our defenses." He paused to let the information sink in. "I don't need to remind all of you that we are under the guns of Keowee. If they rise up against us, we'll be penned up in this fort like cattle. Bring in all the food and livestock that you can round up. Remember, we are now at war. I expect every man to do his duty." He looked towards the small band of militia. "Sergeant Sanders, a word with you. Officers, see to your men.

Dismissed!"

"Come on, Winslow," Sanders said to the lanky man. The two of them marched away while the twenty-odd men left behind milled about muttering amongst themselves. A few of them dropped to the ground and sat cross-legged as they waited.

* * * *

The sergeant motioned to the men as he made his way back. When they gathered 'round, he blew between his lips. "To hell with buryin' those dead men. We're goin' to round up survivors if there are any. Anyone we find we'll bring back here. We'll sneak out at midnight tonight." He chuckled morbidly. "If we *can* sneak out. Damned fort is right in the middle of a Cherokee town. Check your weapons and mounts. Anything you see wrong, fix it! Bring enough food for two days, just in case. Any questions?"

Thomas and Martin exchanged puzzled looks. "What about us, Sergeant?" Thomas said. "Our horses are in no condition for this."

"We've got a couple you can use for the time being. There's plenty of animals around here that their riders won't need anymore. If you know what I mean." He looked at Thomas as he spoke. His meaning was clear. They would inherit the horses of the men claimed by the smallpox epidemic.

Thomas and the other militiamen, however, never left the fort. That night, the Cherokees in Keowee, who had only sporadically participated in the uprising against the British, were joined by the great chieftain, Occonostota and his warriors. Occonostota pressed for an all-out attack. Yet, with the Cherokee hostages still imprisoned inside the fort, the majority of the headmen argued against risking an assault. They preferred to starve the garrison out.

The Cherokees surrounded the fort as soon as it was dark, cutting off its communication with the outside world. Inside the fort, the garrison slept on their arms, expecting to be overwhelmed at any moment.

Loving Lynn Celia

CHAPTER SIXTEEN

Fort Prince George, South Carolina
February 16, 1760

Dawn. Ice crystals, formed from the morning's frozen dew, glittered on the barrels of the cannons. A gentle breeze, blowing in from the northwest, wafted across the river, bringing with it tendrils of wood smoke from the Cherokee village on the far side. Overhead, the Union Jack stirred to life as it was hoisted to the top of the fort's flagpole.

"Dismissed!" the captain barked. The men in the ranks dispersed. Their shoes produced crunching sounds as they made their way across the frozen parade ground. Some moved towards their posts along the walls of the fort, others went in search of breakfast. Thomas stopped and yawned before starting towards the western wall. He could see Winslow Driggers, tall and lanky, eyeing them from the guard walk. With his extra coat and the bright red shawl draped over his hat and tied under his chin, Winslow looked like a child's stuffed doll. He smiled and lifted his hand in greeting.

Thomas waved back. He looked upward at the hills to the northwest. Despite a hazy fog that covered their peaks, they were visible. The thought that Lynn Celia might be crossing them at this very moment flashed through his mind.

Martin stood at his side, his eyes following Thomas's gaze. "Wonderin' 'bout the wife?" he said quietly. He gave Thomas a sympathetic pat on the shoulder. "We'll find her. With all the meanness 'round here, I wouldn't be surprised if she's still somewhere nearby. Those young bucks won't want to miss a fight."

On the northern wall, a sentry turned and shouted for the sergeant of the guard. Men stopped and turned to look, open-mouthed, in his direction. The other sentries stood frozen in place, peering toward the river. Thomas saw one of the sergeants jog to a ladder and climb onto the walkway. He stopped alongside the sentry who had called out the alert and turned to follow the man's pointed finger. Whatever he saw caused him to scamper back to the ground.

"We best get to our posts," Martin quipped. He gave Thomas's arm a tug as he started for the wall. They followed the other militiamen up onto the walkway. At the edge of a large canebrake on the far side of the river, stood the Cherokee Chieftain, Occonostota. As Thomas watched, one of the officers, wearing a redcoat with the green facings of South Carolina's Independent Company,

200

stepped through the sally port and walked, unarmed, down to the riverbank. The two men conferred for only a moment.

The officer spun about and returned to the fort. Captain Coytmore and the other officers of the fort met him at the gate where they stood in a small cluster, talking quietly. Thomas saw the captain shrug his shoulders noncommittally and motion for two of the lieutenants to follow him. At the river, the lieutenants stood, one on each side of the captain, as he parleyed with Occonostota. Each group remained on their side of the river.

Without taking his eyes off of the three men, Thomas whispered to Martin, "What you reckon they're sayin'?" he asked. Martin made a silent gesture with his hand, indicating he had no idea.

Across the river they could see Occonostota holding up a bridle. He said something to the officers and turned to go. Captain Coytmore removed his cocked hat and ran his fingers through his dark, curly hair in a relieved manner. He smiled and said something to one of the lieutenants. All three of the men laughed. As they turned back to the fort, Occonostota waved the bridle in a circular motion over his head in a farewell salute.

"Somethin' ain't right," Martin mumbled.

Before Thomas could reply, the canebrake across the river erupted Cherokees. At least thirty warriors jumped to their feet and fired their muskets at the backs of the three Englishmen. All three of the officers went down. Both of the lieutenants struggled to their feet. Each grabbed an arm of the fallen captain and headed towards the fort. The captain's feet bumped along the ground as they stumbled forward. Even from this distance, Thomas could see that both of the lieutenants had been wounded. The captain looked dead.

Along the wall, muskets boomed. Thomas aimed into the middle of a cluster of warriors and fired. Beside him, Martin picked out a warrior, following his movements before his rifle cracked. The man stumbled, tried to stand erect, then sank to the ground. With a loud whack, a musket ball impacted the inside wall beside Thomas! He looked over his shoulder. All around the fort the woodline was obscured by smoke. "My god!" he exclaimed, "They're all around us."

To his left, a militiaman sank to one knee. The man reached over his shoulder, clawing at his shoulder blade. He had been struck in the back by a ball fired by one of the Cherokees on the far side of the fort. When several of the men turned to run, they were halted by the voice of Sergeant Sanders.

It lashed out at them like a bullwhip, drawing them back to their duty.

"Stand fast!" the sergeant bellowed. "Those Indians over there can't see you, it's just blind luck they hit anything when they overshot their target." He grabbed the fallen man's musket and began reloading. "You two." He pointed at Thomas and Martin. "Get that man to the surgeon."

Leaving their weapons canted against the wall of the stockade, they manhandled the unconscious man down the ladder. On the ground, Martin grabbed the limp form and swung it over his shoulder. "I'll get him to the surgeon," he said. "You get back up there and keep an eye on my rifle!" He stumbled towards the hospital without looking back.

Thomas clambered up the ladder and raced back to his post. The only targets he could see were puffs of gun smoke sprouting from the thick cane along the river. Double-shotting his long-barreled doglock, he pointed it in the direction of the hidden warriors and pulled the trigger, knowing it would be pure luck if he hit anything at that distance.

"Don't waste your time with buckshot." The sergeant cautioned him. "Just load with balls, they'll skip through the cane over there. Maybe you'll get one of the bloody bastards in the leg!"

After twenty minutes, the firing on both sides began to slacken. From one of the bastions a cannon boomed. The ball flew straight across the river and through the Keowee council house. The men on the walls cheered and shook their fists at the figures that poured from its doors and windows in a mad dash to put as much distance between themselves and the doomed building as possible.

For the next few hours, the cannons facing the town continued to fire, sending balls and grapeshot crashing through the cane break and the houses on the far side of the river. All around the village, men, women and children threaded their way towards the safety of the hills. Behind them, the battle degenerated into nothing more than a contest of snipers. Soldiers and militiamen armed with rifles potted across the open area with little effect while the men on both sides hunkered down and waited.

"What news?" several men asked the question of Martin as he returned from the hospital and dropped down alongside Thomas. He shook his head. "The Captain's dead.

He died instantly, they say. Lieutenant Miln is in command now."

"He issued any orders?"

Martin gave a gruff laugh. "Well, he didn't have the time to talk to me," he said.

Below them, a soldier stopped and looked up. "Officer's call at Captain Coytmore's quarters," he said to Sergeant Sanders. "Lieutenant Miln says for you to come and represent the militia." Without waiting for an answer, the soldier moved on to the south wall, where he relayed the order to an officer sitting with his back against the logs and his legs swinging over the side of the walkway.

Sergeant Sanders returned ten minutes later. He stood at the base of the wall, looking up at the faces peering down on him from above. He pointed to two of the men. "Winslow, you and Ozborne come with me," he said. "We've got work to do." He paused for a moment, eyeing the others on the wall before pointing to Martin. "Mr. Grubb, you come along too, I rather think you'll enjoy this."

Thomas watched the four men make their way across the parade ground. As they went, men from other sections of the wall joined them. The belligerent group stopped in front of the small barracks that housed the Cherokee hostages. The fort's blacksmith was already there. He stood to one side of the door, a hammer in his hand and an anvil set atop a round block of wood. Thomas watched as one of the officers gave the men their instructions. When he motioned towards the door of the barracks, a big, burly soldier stepped forward and gave it a hefty shove. It wouldn't budge. The big man stepped back and eyed the door maliciously. Thomas guessed it was being held shut by the hostages inside.

Four of the men separated themselves from the group and disappeared behind the storehouse. They returned carrying a log that they used as a battering ram to force the door off its hinges. The big soldier who had first tried the door stepped inside. He immediately reemerged, stumbling backwards and clawing at a bloody gash in his side. The officer lunged past him, swinging his sword at a Cherokee who appeared in the doorway and driving him back into the cramped building.

Holding the Cherokees inside the building at bay with the point of his weapon, the officer waved the men through the door. They surged inside like a greedy mob. Thomas heard the muffled report of a musket from inside the building. It was followed by two more shots. Martin and two other militiamen pulled their tomahawks and plunged through the opening.

Many of the men manning the walls, seeing what was happening, leapt to the ground and raced over to the barracks to join in the massacre. Howls and curses floated on the air. Thomas watched as one of the regulars dragged an Indian from the building by his foot. The warrior kicked at the soldier with his free foot and held onto the door frame with both hands. The blacksmith jumped forward with his hammer and swung it at the warrior's head. The Cherokee went limp.

Stepping back, the blacksmith wiped the blood from the hammer onto his leather apron. He laughed and said something to the soldier who dropped the man's foot and rolled the body out of the doorway. Both men started when the Cherokee attempted to roll onto his side. The blacksmith looked at the soldier, smiled, gave a slight bow, and offered the hammer to the soldier by laying the handle across the back of his forearm. The soldier took it and straddled the man. He used it to pound the back of the warrior's head into a bloody pulp.

The soldiers and militiamen who had stormed into the cabin began to reappear, dragging the mutilated bodies of the hostages with them. They dumped the bodies in a pile, scalped, dismembered—beaten beyond recognition.

Thomas could hear the angry curses of Lieutenant Miln as he raced across the parade ground, waving his arms wildly to gain the attention of the gang of murderers. Too late, he ordered the men back to their positions. Red-faced, he turned on the officers and sergeants who had taken part in the massacre, berating them for the sheer wantonness of the act—an act that was sure to have dangerous repercussions.

Thomas sat on the wall in stunned silence. He watched as Martin and the other militiamen strolled back across the parade ground. They were laughing and elbowing each other as if they had just taken part in the greatest of jokes. As he walked, Martin shoved two scalps into his hunting bag. When he looked up, and saw Thomas's horrified stare, he winked and gave a quick laugh. Patting the bag he smiled. "Them soldiers over there, tell me North Carolina pays seventy dollars apiece for scalps. This makes five of 'em I've got now. Not bad for a few minutes work!" Thomas turned away and peered through a loophole. On the far side of the river, well out of musket range, he could see a few Cherokees milling about. What would they do when they found out about this? He bowed his head and prayed Lynn Celia was far, far away from Fort Prince George.

"Whose idea was that?" one of the militiamen asked Winslow Driggers when he plopped down onto the sentry walk. Winslow rested his back against the wall and stretched his legs out straight before him. "No one's," he answered. "We was just supposed to put them in irons. But damned if they didn't stab the first man through the door! Then cut on two others. We can't let 'em get away with that, can we?"

Thomas's concern over the deaths of the hostages proved well-founded. Almost every person in the Cherokee nation had lost a friend or a relative in the massacre. Warriors, who had up until now, refrained from making raids on the frontier, rose en masse. Cabin after cabin was burned, their inhabitants slaughtered, or carried off into captivity. Through a dispatch smuggled into the fort by an English trader's Cherokee wife, they learned Ninety-six had beaten off an attack by over two hundred warriors. Other posts had been threatened or destroyed. Fort Loudoun, on the Little Tennessee River, managed to smuggle a message through a hundred and fifty miles of hostile territory. Like Fort Prince George, they were surrounded and under siege. With provisions running low, they faced an uncertain future. Unable to send aid to their besieged comrades, the garrison of Fort Prince George huddled behind their walls and waited for their own relief column to appear.

Loving Lynn Celia

CHAPTER SEVENTEEN

Fort Prince George, South Carolina
June 14, 1760

The Cherokees had no intention of wasting the lives of their warriors by assaulting Fort Prince George. Instead, for four long months, they flitted among the trees and cane breaks, taking pot shots at the garrison. Rarely was anyone injured on either side.

By the middle of June, the garrison's main want was firewood. Wood cutting parties could not be sent outside the range of the sharpshooter's rifles. When the available wood was exhausted, the men began to break up furniture and other non-essential items. As a last resort, they began sawing the top twelve inches off of the logs in the fort's wall.

* * * *

Inside the barracks, Thomas sat on the floor with his back against the wall. There was no other place to sit, the beds and chairs had long since been consumed by the fort's cooking fires. He canted his head to one side and listened for a moment, trying to isolate a distant sound that was barely audible above the rumble of Martin's snoring. He reached out and nudged the sleeping man in the ribs. Martin snorted and rolled onto his side, the snoring stopped. Thomas continued to listen as the sound drew nearer and more distinct. He jumped to his feet and rushed out onto the parade ground. All around him, men were streaming out of the other structures within the fort. On the walls the sentries were leaning outward and shading their eyes as they peered towards the south.

Martin stumbled out of the door behind him, still half-asleep. He paused in the sunlight to pull his shirt on over his head. "I hear bagpipes!" he exclaimed. He laughed and gave Thomas a solid slap on the shoulder. "By God, that can only mean one thing!"

Along with the rest of the garrison, Thomas and Martin scrambled onto the walls. They cheered and waved their hats as the first rank of drummers and pipers marched into view behind an officer mounted on a tall, speckled charger. In the woods to both sides of the slow-moving column, Thomas caught glimpses of militiamen and Rangers gliding from tree to tree as they kept the flanks of the army clear of the enemy. Rank after rank of soldiers marched into view. By the time they were all clear of the forest, Thomas estimated there were close to two thousand men coming to the relief of the fort.

Half of the force halted at the river and fell out of ranks. While those men began setting up tents and gathering wood for fires, the others forded the river and marched into the deserted village on the other side.

While the kilted highlanders searched the town and put it to the torch, mounted Rangers pursued the retreating Cherokees that had scurried away at the first sight of this vast host. They returned at dusk with little more than a few fresh scalps to show for their efforts.

That night, the men of the besieged garrison wandered among the militia camps, searching for familiar faces and for news from the outside world.

As Thomas and Martin strolled through one of the camps, a hand descended on Thomas's shoulder. Startled, he jumped and spun defensively, only to find Cub grinning in his direction. They shook hands warmly.

"Come on over to the fire," Cub said. "There's five of us from Ninety-six over yonder." He made a motion with his hand to indicate a general direction of travel and led the way. They found Christopher Christ and Wiley Jenkins sitting beside two other men they remembered seeing on the muster days at Ninety-Six. Both Christopher and Wiley were hunched over, cross-legged, next to the fire. They were staring into the flames, lost in thought. A jug of rum sat on the ground between them.

Wiley looked up as they sat across from him. He nodded his head in greeting and said, "How do." A slow smile spread across his face. "Haven't seen you in a month of Sundays. Some folks thought you were dead. Find them Cherokees you were after?"

Martin leaned across the fire and plucked the jug from between the two men. He held it up. "Mind?"

"Go 'head," Wiley said. He pulled a small pouch from inside the collar of his shirt and produced a short-stemmed pipe from it. Thomas and Martin watched, desire etched on their faces, as he tamped a pinch of tobacco into the bowl with a grubby finger. The fort's garrison had run out of tobacco a month ago. Their mouths watered as Wiley lit his pipe with a twig from the fire. He took a long, lazy pull and blew the smoke out slowly and luxuriously in their direction. When he handed the pipe across the fire, Thomas took it eagerly and popped it into his mouth. Beside him, Martin turned up the jug. His Adam's apple bobbed greedily as he drank. He held the jug between his legs when he finished drinking and looked towards Wiley. "Nope," he said, wiping his mouth with the back of his hand. "We been cooped up here since February. Ain't seen hide nor hair of her since she was took."

"That's too bad," Wiley said. He held his hand out for the jug. Martin surrendered it grudgingly. "What's the news from home? We heard Ninety-Six was attacked."

Wiley pursed his lips, nodding as he studied the flames for a moment. He looked up and peered at them from across the fire. "It was," he said shifting his gaze to Thomas. "They burned your place to the ground." He made a motion towards Cub with his free hand. "His too."

Cub nodded. "They did." He said it to no one in particular. Off to one side, a man began to snore softly. Cub turned his head in that direction as if studying the source of the sound. "It was bound to happen," he said to Thomas. "At least no one was hurt. We all had enough warning to make it to the stockade at Ninety-Six.

"Where's Eunice and your young'uns?" Thomas asked. He was secure in the knowledge that his family was safe in Augusta.

Cub motioned towards Wiley. "They're with Doc Hatcher. He needed a woman to take care of his house. His indentured woman ran away after the Injuns pulled foot. Some think she was took, but most say she's a runaway." He looked to Wiley. "You knew the woman, what do you say?"

"Runaway," Wiley said. He immediately changed the subject. "You boys planning on goin' home, or commin' with us?"

Thomas picked up a short stick and poked lethargically at the fire. "I reckon I'll go on with the army," he said. "Got no reason to hurry back, and a sight of reasons to head north. At least I'll earn a little hard money to tie me over 'til next spring. When are the soldiers planning on movin' on?"

Cub shrugged his shoulders. "Ain't heard, but knowin' this Colonel Montgomerie, it won't be long. He moves like his ass is on fire. Why, I bet we've burned fifteen towns between here and Ninety-Six in the past month. These highlanders ain't as slow as most regulars."

"Get any Injuns?" Wiley asked.

"At the first town. We killed near sixty. They weren't expecting this bunch to move so fast." He let out a short laugh. "They learned though. After that, every place we came to was deserted."

* * * *

Colonel Montgomerie tarried at Fort Prince George for two weeks, waiting for peace emissaries from the Cherokees to come in for a parley. When they failed to come, he marched his entire command towards the middle Cherokee town of Echoee.

Thomas and the other militiamen from Ninety-Six, rode with the provincial Rangers. They had been thrust out in front of the main army as an advance guard. On the morning of June 26th, they secured a ford across the Chattooga River where they took up positions on each bank to guard the crossing of the regulars. Not a shot had been fired since leaving Fort Prince George, but the signs of hostile Cherokees were everywhere.

Thomas, Martin and Cub sat their mounts on the west bank of the river, watching the regulars in their bright uniforms cross from the South Carolina shore into the colony of Georgia. Martin shook his head. "There's something that just ain't right," he said. "These Cherokees should be nipping at our flanks day and night. I've never seen so much sign and not had at least one brush with their scouts." He reached into his hunting bag and pulled out a twist of tobacco. "I've got a bad feeling that they're leadin' us somewhere we don't want to be."

"Have you said anything to Captain Morrison?" Thomas looked at the other man, watching as he gnawed a chaw of tobacco off of a long, black twist with his back teeth. He inclined his head to the far side of the river where the Ranger Captain sat alongside Colonel Montgomerie. Both officers were engaged in an animated discussion with Patrick Calhoun, one of Morrison's lieutenants. Lieutenant Calhoun sat his mount, facing the two officers; he was gesturing to the army's right flank as he spoke. Thomas saw Montgomerie shake his head and point across the river. Calhoun made a quick reply which Montgomerie ignored, and spun his mount away from the two officers. He splashed through the shallow waters of the ford, stopping to speak with the three Rangers as he passed.

"You men see anything odd, you let me know right away," Calhoun said to them. He removed his cocked hat and pulled a brightly colored kerchief from inside the crown. He used it to wipe his forehead clean. "I think we're ridin' into a heap of trouble." He replaced the kerchief and popped the hat back into place, said, "Let's go," and rode to the west.

"That boy has some good instincts." Martin quipped as they watched the young officer ride away. "He'll make a good Indian fighter if he lives long enough."

The men turned their horses and followed the lieutenant along the trail. The majority of the Rangers were already well ahead of the column. Fanned out to the north, east and west, they ranged along the crests of the mountains on each side of the army.

The lieutenant drew his mount to a halt and slid from the saddle. He knelt in the road studying a set of tracks as Thomas and the other two men rode up. They halted, watching as he moved from one side of the trail to the other in search of signs. He pointed to a pair of tracks cutting across the trail.

"See this?" he said, without looking up. "These tracks ain't over fifteen minutes old. They cut right across my own tracks from when I passed this way heading to the river." He looked up at the mountainside and mumbled to himself, "They can't be to the top yet." He shaded his eyes, trying to pick out signs of the enemy scouts clambering along the slopes above. He made a disgusted sound and shook his head.

When Martin spoke, he looked up.

"You've got the same feelin' I have, haven't you?" Calhoun said.

Martin nodded. "Yes, sir. I've been on a lot of Indian campaigns, and I ain't never seen any of 'em that would let an army just march into their territory like this without raisin' some fuss over it. I think we're ridin' into a big ambush somewhere up ahead."

"I do too, but the Colonel thinks they're too scared to tangle with his men." He slapped the palm of one hand with the ends of his reins while he thought. "Can't blame him, though. The Cherokees have fled in a panic from every town we've come to." Martin scoffed. "They ain't scared of no one in this army. That panic's just a ruse. No sir, we're being watched every step of the way."

Calhoun swung into his saddle and looked towards Cub. "Ride back and report this to the colonel. Tell him it's just a few young warriors lookin' to pick off a straggler or two. Have him warn his soldiers to stay close in to the column."

* * * *

The army wound its way forward, inching along the narrow path, often chopping its way through tangled underbrush in those places where the trail closed in on itself. By late afternoon, they had come to the gap that led to the middle Cherokee towns. They marched north, following the path leading them straight to Echoee. It lay about twenty miles ahead.

They rode along the stony banks of a narrow, swiftly flowing stream as they urged their mounts upward and across a slight roll of land situated between two tall mountains. At the top of the rise, the Rangers paused to study the steep-sided ridges stretching along each side of the pass for as far as they could see.

Lieutenant Calhoun pointed out a campsite that would hold the entire army when it caught up to them. He gave instructions that pushed half of the Rangers out into a wide arc to the north to guard against any sizable force of Cherokees lurking in the area. As these men rode away, he pointed to a level clearing in the center of the campsite where the army's mounts would be picketed and detailed a handful of men to set it up. The remaining men scattered to gather firewood.

That night, the Rangers sat around their fire discussing the odd behavior of the enemy. Many of the older men agreed with Martin and Lieutenant Calhoun, believing an ambush was somewhere ahead.

"I don't like it," the lieutenant said. "Sure as I'm sittin' here, the Cherokees are waitin' for us. With all the signs we've been seein', they must have at least a thousand warriors." He pointed his finger at Martin and waved it back and forth, so that the gesture included Thomas and Cub. "I want you three ridin' up front with the captain tomorrow." He looked from right to left, surveying the dark outlines of the tall mountains on either side. "It's open through here, but up ahead, unless I miss my guess, it's going to narrow. When it does, look out. There's where they'll hit us."

One of the men sitting in the darkness beyond the circle of firelight, spoke up. "It's been mighty narrow for the past thirty miles, lieutenant. Why haven't they hit us?"

"Like you said. It was narrow for thirty miles. They wouldn't have been able to do anything but stop us. They want to destroy us." He made a motion with one hand to indicate the area around them. "Here, if they can hit us in a narrow pass and drive us back, we'll be spread out all over this level area. Easy pickin's if we don't stay together."

Martin nodded soberly. "Makes perfect sense," he said.

* * * *

The army moved forward before daylight. Colonel Montgomerie's plan was to make a rush towards Echoee before the enemy realized what was happening. Captain Morrison led the way. Thomas, Cub and Martin rode single-file behind him. Twenty other Rangers were spread out to each side. They moved ahead cautiously.

Five miles from the camp, just as Lieutenant Calhoun had predicted, the mountains closed in, channeling the men into a level area along the banks of a muddy river. They followed the river north. Along both of its banks the brush and cane breaks grew thicker. Soon the Rangers were swallowed by thickets so dense they couldn't see more than twenty feet in any one direction. Sensing danger, they halted and warily surveyed the undergrowth ahead. On each side they could hear the faint rustling of movement. Behind them, they could hear the sounds of the main army as it accordioned in on itself and came to a halt.

Colonel Montgomerie, flanked by his aides, came riding forward at a gallop. He stopped to talk with Captain Morrison. "This is it, Captain," he said. "If I were the enemy, this is where I would strike. Spread your men out and move forward, slow and careful. I'll follow with the main column.

If they attack, you hold them in place. We'll circle around to the right and pin them against this river. It's not much, but it will scatter their warriors if we can flush them into it." Montgomerie returned Morrison's salute and cantered back to the main column.

The Rangers sat their mounts looking from man to man, gauging what each would do in the upcoming crisis. The Captain motioned for them to spread out and waved them forward. In the heavy brush it was impossible to see more than three or four of the men at any one time. Thomas followed behind and to one side of the captain. His stomach felt as if it were tied into a knot, he wiped his sweaty palms on the sides of his breeches and pulled the hammer of his old doglock to full cock. Up ahead, he saw movement. His eyes widened as he recognized the form of a man rising from a nest of twisted cane. Before anyone could react, the man leveled his musket and fired. The entire canebrake burst into flame. Captain Morrison somersaulted over the withers of his horse. He hit the ground hard, directly in front of Thomas.

CHAPTER EIGHTEEN

Itseyi Gap, North Carolina
June 27, 1760

Holding one hand against his wounded side, the captain staggered to his feet. A second musket ball hit him high in the left shoulder, rocking him back onto his heels.

Thomas spurred his mount forward. Throwing his musket to his shoulder he fired a load of buckshot into the underbrush, then reached down and grabbed the back of the captain's hunting frock, pulling him face down over the front of his saddle. He could hear the wounded man groan as he spun his mount around and raced to safety. Around him, the other Rangers leapt from their saddles and sought cover. From behind downed trees and a few scattered rocks, they exchanged fire with the unseen Cherokees.

Arrows and musket balls zipped through the air as Thomas broke free of the thick cane. He emerged in front of a long row of light infantrymen who were advancing in a line towards the sound of the battle. A company of Grenadiers in high miter caps followed closely on their heels. Seeing the wounded man slung across his saddle, both lines parted to let him pass.

Behind the Grenadiers, Thomas reined in alongside the regimental surgeon and Colonel Montgomerie. Both men were studiously observing the deployment of the troops. The Colonel was pointing out positions and bellowing orders. Off to one side, two orderlies were scurrying about and setting up a makeshift hospital. They jumped forward to grab the wounded man as soon as they saw him. Thomas let the captain's limp form slide into their hands.

Montgomerie glanced at the dying officer. "Who's in charge up there?" He had to shout to be heard over the din of musketry erupting all along their front.

"Lieutenant Calhoun, sir!" Thomas stole a quick glance over his shoulder, anxious to return to his friends. The Colonel reached out and rested a hand on his forearm. He leaned forward to make himself heard. "Tell the lieutenant his men must engage the enemy and hold them in place. I will send the Royals to the right where they can fire into the enemy's flank. Understand?"

Thomas gave a quick nod. "Yes, sir."

"Good man." The colonel gave his arm a fatherly pat. "Good luck to you."

Back in the thicket, Thomas threw the reins of his animal to one of the Rangers left behind to guard the horses. The rest of the men had already disappeared into the underbrush, closing in on the enemy with muskets, knives and tomahawks.

Thomas moved forward slowly, guiding himself by the sounds of the battle. Here and there, the body of one of the Rangers was sprawled in death. When he heard the sharp crack of a rifle, he moved towards it, knowing it had to be a Ranger. The dull thuds of the muskets could be coming from either side. He almost stumbled over Martin who was lying in the grass behind a low outcropping of stone. Cub stood off to one side with his back against a bullet-scarred tree. He looked towards Thomas and grinned as he rammed a load of buckshot down the muzzle of his fowling piece.

"The captain dead?" Martin asked as Thomas knelt at his side and searched for a target. Before he could answer, an arrow slapped the stock of his musket with a solid whack! It ricocheted into the brush behind him. Thomas dropped to the ground and rolled behind the moldering remains of a downed oak.

"Better keep low." Martin cautioned. "There must be five hundred of 'em out there."

A second arrow thumped into the log in front of Thomas. He slid lower, cradling his musket in both arms. To his right, Cub peeked from behind the tree. He spotted a target, jerked his fowling piece to his shoulder, and fired. He jumped back behind the tree and punched the air with his fist. "Got 'em!"

Thomas reached over the log and pulled the arrow free. He studied the cane shaft. It was a hunting arrow tipped with an obsidian arrowhead and fletched with turkey feathers. He lay the arrow to one side, it would make a fine trophy to take back to Richard. The thought of his son flooded his memory with images of Lynn Celia. Where was she? Maybe, just up ahead in the Cherokee town of Echoee. Thomas felt a sudden, irresistible urge to move forward and race to the village. It would be deserted of warriors at a time like this. If she were there…

The trunk of the downed tree exploded into splinters, jolting him back into the present. He peered over the tree and saw the smoke of the Cherokee's musket, not fifteen yards away. Rising to one knee, he took aim, and fired into it. Without waiting to see the result of his shot, he sank back onto his side and began reloading.

The Rangers and the Cherokees continued to fight stubbornly. Behind them, they could hear the sounds of the light infantry fighting its way through the thick brush, followed by the grenadiers and Highlanders. Passing through the ranks of the Rangers, they plunged ahead with their bayonets held at the ready. To the right, the dull thuds of musket fire grew in intensity as the Royal Scots moved onto the right flank. Off to the east, unseen by the Rangers, the Scots spread out along a slight rise and turned inward, plunging into the flank of the enemy with their bayonets.

Thomas could hear the shouts and screams of defiance as the two sides struggled, unseen, in the thickets. Lieutenant Calhoun shouted for the Rangers to move to the left where they could shoot down the retreating Cherokees as the regulars flushed them from the cover of the thickets and into the muddy waters of the Little Tennessee River.

The retreating Cherokees rushed across the open water with such agility most of the Rangers had time for only one shot before their targets clambered into the underbrush and disappeared on the far side of the river. Once across, they turned and renewed the fight. The Royal Scots, Highlanders, light infantry, and Grenadiers, all intermixed with each other, appeared on the east bank and plunged into the muddy water in pursuit of the warriors. Lieutenant Calhoun ordered the Rangers to follow.

The Rangers were crossing in single file when they were halted in midstream by a shout from Colonel Montgomerie. Thomas and Lieutenant Calhoun turned to look back and stood waiting in the waist-deep water as the Colonel coaxed his mount into the sluggish current. He halted alongside him, oblivious to the stray balls flying through the air and skipping along the water.

He looked down at the two Rangers. "Lieutenant Calhoun, these Indians are staying in contact with us with the intention of luring us to the west, away from their town. I want you and your Rangers to mount up and ride towards Echoee. I will reform the army and follow you. The Indians will either move to block our advance or they'll race ahead of us to gather up their women and children. If you reach the village ahead of us, burn it to the ground and scatter any warriors you find there."

Thomas's heart leapt into his throat. He found it almost impossible to contain himself as he thought of the possibility of finding Lynn Celia. "I'll inform the men," he volunteered. He slogged his way to the far bank, shouting at the top of his lungs and motioning for the Rangers to return to their horses.

* * * *

Thomas, Martin, and Cub followed behind Lieutenant Calhoun. The remainder of the Rangers trotted along, two abreast, to the rear. Ahead, through the tree trunks of the thinning forest, they caught their first fleeting glimpse of Echoee, the first of the Cherokee Middle Towns. They urged their mounts from the trees, stopping at the edge of a field of half-grown corn. The town stood at the center of a large clearing. It was a small town, containing no more than twenty houses. On the far side of the town, Thomas could see a handful of tiny figures as they scurried from their homes and disappeared into the corn field to the north. The Rangers made no attempt to overtake them; one ambush in a day was enough for them.

Martin walked his mount forward, stopping alongside the lieutenant. "Are you takin' us in there?" he asked. From the inflection in his voice it was clear he thought it a bad idea.

The lieutenant eyed Martin for a moment before he spoke. "I think not," he said. "We've accomplished our mission by drawing the enemy away from the main army. It would be foolhardy to risk being trapped in there if those warriors come back."

Thomas's mouth dropped open. "But..." he fell silent when the lieutenant's head swung around. "I know the story of your wife, Mr. Simpson, and you have my deepest sympathies. But, the fact remains, to risk being caught in that town by almost a thousand warriors is pure suicide."

Thomas took a deep breath. "Sir, with all due respect. We should fire a few of the buildings if we do nothing else. If the Cherokees haven't already broken off from the main army, that'll bring them here at a run."

The lieutenant cast a skeptical eye at the woods to their rear. The other Rangers sat their mounts silently. A few had detached themselves from the group and were riding along the edge of the corn field, searching for signs of any enemy lurking nearby. One methodically slashed off the tassels of the corn stalks with a saber.

Lieutenant Calhoun gave Thomas a quick smile. He motioned to a sergeant who rode forward.

"Sergeant Floyd, you will take twenty men and enter the town. Fire the buildings and return here with all possible speed. The rest of the company will dismount and wait here until you return."

"I'm goin' with you," Thomas said immediately. Cub and Martin also volunteered. The sergeant smiled, pointed out the other volunteers, and led the small group forward. They cantered across the field, trampling the tender shoots of corn beneath their horses' hooves. All twenty men had their weapons held at the ready as they zigzagged through the tight cluster of buildings. Except for a handful of scruffy dogs that slinked away as the riders approached, the town was deserted. Several of the men dismounted and began rifling through the buildings. "Leave the loot, damn it!" the sergeant snapped. "Just set a few fires and let's get the hell outta here."

Leaving their mounts in Cub's charge, Thomas and Martin raced from building to building. Sticking their heads into the openings they made a quick scan of the interior as they called Lynn Celia's name. If they heard nothing, they moved on. The other Rangers, well aware of Thomas's story, helped in the search. Minutes dragged by, five, then ten, then fifteen.

"That's enough," the sergeant thought aloud. He began to bellow orders. "Harnage," he said, pointing to a ranger who had just stepped from the doorway of a cabin. "Drop the damned dress and set fire to that building." The man stopped and grinned up at him. He stuffed the dress he had pilfered into his hunting pouch and stepped back through the door. He reappeared a few moments later. Behind him a slight tendril of smoke curled upward from between the shingles of the roof.

"Let's go men!" the sergeant roared at the top of his voice. "That smoke'll bring 'em here at a run. 'Less you want to burn with the town, mount up!"

Men boiled from the huts and cabins of the town. Swinging into their saddles, they stuffed all manner of plunder into their hunting shirts and saddle bags. Clothing, tools, and a few assorted weapons were carted from the houses; one man even carried a spinning wheel. Holding it in one hand, he guided his mount back into ranks with the others. The Rangers laughed and pointed, some made derisive sounds in the direction of the more overzealous plunderers as they formed up and headed back across the cornfield.

The man with the spinning wheel shook it in their direction. "Laugh if you want too," he taunted them. "I've got a wife and four young'uns at home that have need of this."

Thomas followed at the rear of the column. Having found no trace of Lynn Celia, he was sullen and withdrawn. He kept looking back over his shoulder, hoping to see her break from the cover of the far tree line and run, shouting and laughing, into his arms.

After the army had turned towards the village, the Cherokees had broken off the battle and fled in the direction of Nikwasi, a large town four miles north of Echoee. They were anxious to move their women and children out of harm's way. Many of the survivors from the lower towns had painted vivid pictures of what they had witnessed when Montgomerie's forces marched into their towns. The warriors of Nikwasi had no wish to go through the same heartbreak. As they neared Echoee, a small group of warriors in the lead threw up their hands and halted. Ahead, they could hear the rumble of approaching riders. They scattered; many sprinted up a steep hillside and took up positions looking down on the trail below. As they waited, they cast worried looks to the north, where a plume of oily black smoke was climbing into the still air.

Some of the younger hot heads screamed defiance at the Rangers and opened fire the instant the plunder-laden riders burst into view. Before the Rangers could react, the entire mountainside belched flame and smoke.

The Rangers turned and scattered, leaving four of their comrades sprawled on the trail. One, laying beside a broken spinning wheel, moved feebly and groaned.

CHAPTER NINTEEN

Little Tennessee River, North Carolina
June 27, 1760

After several hours of dodging small parties of Cherokees wandering throughout the valley, Thomas, Cub, and Martin rejoined the main column. Casualties had been heavy. Wounded men lay in rows as the overworked surgeons and their orderlies worked to amputate shattered limbs and staunch the blood seeping from untreated wounds. The dead lay where they had fallen. Groups of soldiers detailed as gravediggers wandered the battlefield digging shallow graves beside the corpses and rolling them in. A guard of five soldiers watched over each burial squad as they worked. In the west, the sun had dipped below the ridgeline of the mountains; soon it would be too dark to continue the burials.

Lieutenant Calhoun gave a shout of triumph when he saw the three men riding into camp. He strolled over with a smile on his face. "We had just about given up hope," he said, patting Thomas's horse on the neck.

"How's Captain Morrison?" Thomas asked.

The lieutenant frowned. "The captain's dead," he said. Stepping back, he pointed to the Rangers' bivouac area. "The rest of the troop is over there. Go have a bite to eat. Tell the men I'll be over in a bit to tell them what the colonel plans for tomorrow."

After giving their lathered mounts a good feed and rub down, the three men ambled into the pale circle of light cast by the Rangers' fire. Those Rangers not assigned guard or scout duty lounged around the campfire, passing jugs of rum from man to man. Thomas, Cub, and Martin elbowed their way into the circle and dropped to the ground. Martin intercepted one of the jugs and turned it up. He belched and passed it on. "What's the news?" he asked and belched again.

One of the men shrugged. "We're still waitin' on the lieutenant," he said. He motioned towards the river where a small group of officers were standing. Colonel Montgomerie was bent over a folding table, studying a map in the dim glow of a candle lantern. When the meeting ended, the lieutenant turned and walked towards them, as slump-shouldered as a tired old man. One of the sergeants offered him a jug of rum. He took it with a nod of thanks, had a long pull, and called for the men to gather around the fire.

He cleared his throat and began speaking. "We've sustained about a hundred casualties today. In order to carry them, we'll need to use our packhorses. That means the supplies they carry will have to be consumed or destroyed." He paused and took a deep breath. "That creates another problem. If we destroy the supplies and carry the wounded, we won't have enough food to forge ahead. We'll have barely enough left to get back to Fort Prince George." He paused to let the information sink in. "To make matters worse, the Cherokees are not beaten. They'll pull back to the next good spot for an ambush and wait. And from there, to another." A discontented murmuring began to make its way through the ranks as the men guessed what the lieutenant was about to say. One of the bolder men spoke up. "Lieutenant, are you tellin' us we're going to tuck tail and run?"

The lieutenant gave a thin smile. "Not tuck tail and run, no. But with everything considered, the Colonel has decided we'll begin withdrawing first thing in the morning. Tonight, I want each sergeant to go to the commissary and draw as many provisions as his men can eat. Stuff yourselves. Remember, whatever we don't eat, we'll have to destroy before leaving tomorrow.

"What about the rum?" someone shouted from the darkness outside the circle of men. The lieutenant laughed. "No rum. We'll leave it for the Cherokees." A roar of disapproval went up from every throat. "Hold it, men." The lieutenant threw up his hand. "You want them hounding us all day tomorrow?" He pointed to Martin and several of the other experienced Indian fighters in the group. "What does an Indian do when he gets rum?"

"Why, they get drunk as skunks, sir!" one of the men answered. A sly grin spread across his face as he realized what the officer's strategy was. He bellowed good-naturedly. "Well, I'll be. You got this all planned out." He turned as he spoke, addressing the angry, milling men. "If them Indians get aholt of that rum, they'll be three days comin' after us. I hate to give good liquor to those damned murderers, but it sure beats gettin' your skull split by a tomahawk."

That night, the men gorged themselves on the excess supplies. Unable to sleep, many of them sat around their fires, staring into the flames as they thought of home. Others began to gamble. Thomas, never a man for games of chance, watched as Martin dealt a game of cards onto a saddle blanket. Thomas couldn't hear the words of the four men as the game progressed, but he could tell by the actions of the players that Martin and his partner were doing well. One of the men picked up his cards, sneered, and threw them onto the blanket in disgust. He shook his head and jumped to his feet. Stomping over to his saddle, he dropped to one knee and rummaged through his hunting bag, setting its contents onto the ground beside his bedroll. Finding what he was looking for, he jumped to his feet and flapped a crumpled woman's dress to straighten it out. It was bright blue.

Thomas was on his feet almost before the man could turn around. He jerked the garment from the startled man and studied it, wide-eyed. "Where did you get this?" he demanded. He shook the dress in the man's face and repeated his question.

"What's it to you?" the man stammered. Thomas gave the man a shove that caused him to stumble backwards. Tripping over his saddle, he flopped to the ground. He was back on his feet in an instant, ready to fight. By this time, several other men had intervened; they grabbed the two men and dragged them apart. One of the sergeants jumped up from his bed beside the fire and stepped between the two men.

"What's the meaning of this?" the sergeant asked. Thomas felt Martin's grip on his arms ease; he jerked himself free and held the dress up.

"This dress belonged to my wife." He looked past the sergeant to the other man who stood, slack-jawed to one side. The man dusted off the back of his breeches. "I got it in the village today," he said in a surly tone.

"Which house? Come here, draw me a map and show me." When the man hesitated, Thomas apologized. "I'm sorry, you gave me quite a start, pulling it out so sudden. It belongs to my wife. She was taken by the Cherokees back in February." When the man still hesitated, Thomas added, "Please."

The other Rangers came to Thomas's aid. Verbally abusing the man for not helping a fellow ranger, a few of them shoved him and muttered obscenities. Red-faced, the man looked down at his shoes before agreeing to help.

He knelt beside the fire and used a stick to draw a plan of the village. "It was this one right here," he said, pointing out the house he had found the dress in. Thomas nodded and looked up at Martin. "I can't leave with her being this close. I'm staying."

Martin shook his head. "Are you crazy? Its crawling with Indians out there just waiting to lift your hair."

"You said it yourself. By noon tomorrow, they'll all be roaring drunk. What better time to ride out and find Lynn Celia?"

"This is not a good idea, Thomas." Martin looked towards Cub for support. Cub agreed, but volunteered to stay if Thomas did.

Martin ran his fingers through his hair, brushing it back from his forehead. "Thomas, you don't even know if she's there. Her dress could have been traded all over the Cherokee nation before it got here."

"But I've got to know. Where else can I look?" Thomas's voice sounded almost pleading. "I'm staying and I can use your help."

Martin shook his head. "I can't believe I'm doing this, but I'll stay with you." He thought for a moment before adding, "This could work. With only the three of us out there, we'll be hard to spot, and the Cherokees will be so busy followin' the army back to Fort Prince George, this place will be deserted for the next few months." He glanced in Cub's direction. "You better head back, you've got a wife and young'uns to look after. I'm on my own."

Thomas laid his hand on Cub's shoulder. "He's right, you know. Two are as good as a hundred in this situation. The fewer tracks we leave the better chance we'll have of gettin' out of here in one piece. You go on back to Eunice. We'll see you in a couple of months—or not at all."

CHAPTER TWENTY

Ninety-Six, South Carolina
August 29, 1760

Thomas and Martin rode through the rainy night, filthy and slump-shouldered after two months of dodging Cherokee warriors on trails and mountains as far north as Virginia. They reined their mounts in alongside the small cabin that stood to one side of Doc Hatcher's home and slid from their saddles into the ankle-deep muck of the yard. A pale, yellow light grew on the oiled paper of a single window as a lantern flickered to life inside the cabin. The door inched open, the barrel of a musket appeared, followed by the faintly illuminated face of Cub Hall. Cub held the lantern high, shedding its light across their bearded faces. His mouth dropped slightly as recognition set in. "Well, I'll be!" he said. "I thought you two were dead." He turned and spoke over his shoulder. "It's Thomas and Martin," he said to his wife. He lowered the barrel of the musket. Waving them forward, he stood to one side and ushered them into the single room of the small structure. Once inside, they stood to one side of the opening and beat their hats against their thighs to drive out the water before hanging them on wall pegs beside the door.

Thomas untied the frayed and faded sash of his hunting frock and draped it over his hat. He made a motion with his head in the direction of the fireplace. "Mind if I dry out a bit?" he said, moving to stand before the handful of dull embers still glowing in the hearth.

Eunice, wrapped in a blanket, stirred the coals to life and threw a handful of lighter over them. As the fire burst to life, she fed pieces of pine into it and swung an iron kettle, suspended on a crane, over the flames. "I'll have something warmed up for you in a minute," she said. Setting two wooden trenchers on a puncheon table, she stood by her husband's shoulder as Thomas told his story.

"After we left the army, we lay out beneath an overhang about halfway up that tall mountain to the right of the battlefield. We could hear the Cherokees howling like a bunch of bleeding hounds in the valley below. They had a couple of prisoners they had taken from among the Royal Scots." He paused for a moment, thinking of the cries of agony and the smell of burning flesh that drifted as high as their hiding place. The Cherokees had turned back an entire British army. They had been drunk on both victory and rum. "During the night, we crept along the crest of the mountains and descended into the valley just south of Nikwasi. It's a town three or four miles north of Echoee, you know, the one we burned the day of the battle. It's got a big mound in the center and looked important, so we found a hill where we could lay out and look the place over. We lingered there for two days, using the spyglass Lieutenant Calhoun gave us to watch the people there. We didn't see anything, not a single white captive. We skirted around the town, keeping to those tall mountains to the east. About four miles north of Nikwasi, we came on another town. We found out later the Cherokees call it Watauga. We stayed there a few days and then moved north to a huge town named Cowee. We were there nigh on a week, I'm certain I glimpsed Lynn Celia once, but Martin ain't so sure it was her. We were almost spotted, so we high-tailed it into one of the side valleys and held up a few days. When we figured it was safe, we moved back. After another couple of days without seein' anything, we headed up towards Virginia, stopping to spy on any towns we came to on the way." Thomas paused to take a long swill of rum from a wooden noggin before continuing. "A couple of weeks ago, we were about twenty miles south of the town of Taliquo when we happened on a red-headed woman wanderin' in the woods. She told us she had escaped from a massacre up north. It was her that told us about the garrison at Fort Loudoun. It seems they had surrendered with the promise of safe passage back to South Carolina a few days before. They had turned over the fort and marched south.

The next morning, a horde of warriors fell on them. She thinks most of those folks were killed. She escaped with her husband, but he had been hit in the back by an arrow. He died two days later." Thomas shook his head and sighed. "With her to look out for, we headed east until we came out of the mountains, then moved south, skirting the Cherokee lands 'til we came to a settlement. We left the woman with some of her relatives up in North Carolina five days ago." He paused and closed his eyes. "Eunice, hungry as I am, I think I'll skip supper and just curl up over there in the corner and get some sleep if you don't mind."

"You two go right ahead," Cub said. "I'll tend to your horses."

* * * *

Five days later, Thomas headed to Augusta. He stopped at Simpson's Meadow where he spent a day wandering through the burned-out clearing, reliving the memories of happier days. Around the spring, he found the signs of several war parties that had used the clearing as a staging area during their rampages a few months before. Stumbling over the broken and weather-beaten remains of Patience's spinning wheel, he stood and stared down at it for almost an hour as he remembered another one, much like it, lying beside the fallen body of one of the Rangers in Itseyi Pass. With a sigh, he gathered up the broken pieces and dusted them off before tying them into a tight bundle that he strapped behind his saddle. He stayed long enough to dig through the ashes of the cabin and barn, salvaging ax heads and other tools that had survived the flames.

Before leaving, he collected Champ's scattered bones and wrapped them in a blanket. He placed the small bundle in the bottom of a pit at the edge of the meadow and covered them over. He didn't mark the grave.

Loving Lynn Celia

CHAPTER TWENTY-ONE

Savannah River
December 15, 1760

Thomas stood on the bow of the flatboat, deftly steering it free of snags and floating debris as they floated down the rain-swollen Savannah River. On the roof of the crew's cabin, one man stood sentry, a long rifle in his hands as he kept a close watch on both banks of the river. So far, there had been no attacks on the boats working the river between Augusta and Savannah, but no one was willing to leave anything to chance.

After an absence of several years, Thomas's shoulders, arms, and back had ached and stiffened as he awakened long-dormant muscles he seldom used for farming or riding. Now, after three months of poling, any discomfort was long past. Since his return to the river, he rarely spoke. The crew had come to consider him as introverted and sullen and had taken to leaving him to his own silent memories. He was quick to fight and deadly in his anger; only the *Ringtailed Roarers* among the river men dared to challenge him, and when they did, it often turned into a bloody affair. In a few short months, his reputation as a merciless brawler had been established.

As they came abreast of Hutchinson's Island, several of the crew set their poles and nudged the flatboat alongside the *Meg*. With years of experience, the lines were tossed and the cranes were swung out to receive the valuable bales of deerskins and furs collected from across the colony by native hunters during the past winter. The war with the Cherokees had strangled off a large area of prime hunting territory, creating a shortage of the much sought-after skins and causing the prices to skyrocket.

Whatever flaws Lynn Celia's abduction had brought out in Thomas, drink was not one of them. He hoarded his share of the flatboat's profit, banking it in Savannah with his uncle. He planned on moving back into the Cherokee territory as soon as the war ended, armed with enough trade goods to buy his wife's freedom, if she could be found.

After stowing the cargo aboard the *Meg*, the flatboat pushed off. The crew poled alongside a Savannah wharf. With their pay clinking in their pockets, they hopped ashore as soon as they were tied up and headed for the waterfront taverns. Thomas elected to stay on the boat while his father reported to Morgan and arranged for the loading of trade goods in the morning.

That evening, Thomas returned from a quick meal at one of the riverfront taverns. He stretched out on one of the hard bunks in the flatboat's cabin with his head cupped in both hands, staring up at the dull designs of reflected moonlight dancing across the ceiling. He drifted to sleep. He dreamed of Lynn Celia.

He woke with a start. A loud thump at the bow of the vessel had awakened him. It was the unmistakable sound of feet landing on the wooden planks of the deck. Thomas lay quietly listening for the approach of the stranger. More than likely, it was one of the crewmen returning. With no cargo onboard, there was little chance of someone attempting to rob the boat. Yet it never hurt to be careful. Thomas sat up in the bunk. Rotating his body slowly, he set his feet softly on the deck. He grabbed the old brass blunderbuss from under the bunk and flipped the frizzen forward. Unable to see in the dark, he felt the priming with his thumb before closing the flashpan. Outside, a board creaked with that sinister sound a person makes when trying to remain undetected. Thomas backed against the wall, waiting.

The sounds of stealthy movement continued. Thomas could follow the progress of the stranger as he made his way along the starboard side of the vessel by the sounds of his steps on the decking of the narrow walkway.

A sudden rap against the door startled Thomas, almost causing him to pull the trigger of the blunderbuss. After a slight pause, another round of pounding followed.

"Open up, damn it!" The familiar voice of Martin Grubb called. "Thomas, I know you're in there."

With a sigh, Thomas lowered his weapon. "Damn it Martin! Come on in, it's not locked."

He lay the blunderbuss on the bed and fumbled in the half-darkness for a tinderbox as Martin pushed the door open. "And holler out next time. I almost shot you."

"Never mind the candle," Martin said. "We can sit outside. There's almost a full moon to see by."

The two friends sat atop the ship's cabin, their legs dangling over its side as they chatted about the last few months of their lives. After Thomas left Ninety-Six, Martin had returned to Fort Prince George where he rejoined the Rangers. Without any active campaigns being conducted, he was serving as a messenger between Charleston and other areas of military importance. He had arrived in Savannah yesterday to deliver a sealed message to Georgia's governor, Henry Ellis, from Governor Bull of South Carolina. That, he told Thomas, is when he had spied the *Meg* riding at anchor. Recognizing the name of the boat from the stories Thomas had told him, he had bought rum for some of its crewmen. It didn't take long to find out where Thomas was.

"How long are you going to be in Savannah?" Thomas asked after Martin had told his story.

Martin shrugged. "As long as it takes. Sometimes a day, sometimes a week. These governors are peculiar people. They move at their own pace." "Have you heard anything about captives?" Thomas asked.

"Yes, I have."

Thomas sat bolt upright, listening closely as Martin continued. "Some of the other survivors from Fort Loudoun have made their way in. That's what I came by to tell you. One of the women made it through. She claims she saw Lynn Celia." He inhaled, rolled his lips in on themselves and blew the air out through his nose. "She says she was held in the same town as your wife for a few days before the warrior that claimed her took her away."

Thomas turned to Martin, spouting questions faster than the other man could answer them. "What town was she in? When was it? Did she say anything?"

Martin smiled and looked sideways at Thomas. "You plannin' on goin' back up there right this second?" He motioned with his head towards the land of the Cherokees.

Thomas made a series of shallow nods with his head as he thought. "Of course! Just as soon as I can. I've been saving everything I earn for this. My uncle has two warriors from the Upper Creeks willing to take the goods to the Cherokees and make an offer for her. We were just waitin' 'til we knew where she is." Unable to control himself, Thomas jumped to the deck of the flatboat and danced a quick jig. "Come on," he called over his shoulder as he climbed up onto the pier. "Let's go tell my father and uncle!"

* * * *

Morgan and Richard sat in the parlor that had served as a wedding chapel for Thomas and Lynn Celia four short years before. They both listened in silence as Martin told his story.

When Martin finished, Morgan, sitting in a plush leather chair, leaned forward and knocked the cold ashes from his pipe into the palm of his hand. He stood and tossed them into the fire crackling in the hearth. The other three men watched and waited as he made mental calculations and mulled over his next words. He turned his head and peered at Martin over one shoulder. "How accurate do you think this information is?"

He made a slight gesture with his hands. "It is already two months old."

Martin nodded. "True. But there hasn't been much goin' on up there since Montgomerie's expedition pulled back to Charleston and sailed away." He wrapped the fingers of his right hand around his left thumb in a meditative gesture Thomas had grown accustomed to seeing him use when in deep thought. When the problem was particularly vexing, he chewed on his lower lip. Martin nodded and said, "I think she's still in the same town." "Which one was that, again?" Morgan asked.

Martin said, "Cowee," and sat back in his chair. "Up past the gap. Just where Thomas was sure he saw her when we were up there."

Morgan nodded. "Very well. I'll send two Muscogees I trust up there. They're neutral in all of this and should be able to move through the Cherokee towns without much trouble." He turned his attention to Thomas. "As soon as we get the flatboat loaded with our goods tomorrow, we'll pile in enough trade goods for you to get her back."

Thomas opened his mouth to speak, but Morgan waved him into silence. "I know what you're going to say, but we'll talk about the cost later. For the moment, the most important thing is getting your wife back, safe and sound."

CHAPTER TWENTY-TWO

Currahee Mountain, Georgia Colony
January 20, 1761

Thomas threw a small twig into the cooking fire. After watching it burst into flames, he stood and looked over the small camp with a bored and impatient attitude. He was feeling uneasy. The two Muscogee guides had left him, his brother Matthew, and Cub at the base of Currahee Mountain's rocky face. Their camp was beneath a low overhang, invisible to anyone overhead and well off the paths used by the Cherokees in the area. The two Muscogees had been gone for almost ten days. Thomas was beginning to worry. Lost in thought, he began to pace back and forth across the small area.

Cub clapped a hand on Thomas's shoulder, halting him in his tracks. "Don't fret so," he said. "We knew this was going to take some time."

Thomas nodded. "I'm just gettin' antsy, wondering when she'll be back." He indicated their small, almost smokeless fire with a slight jerk of his head. "And we can't stay in one spot forever. The Cherokees who aren't raiding the settlements are out on the hunt this time of the year. It's only a matter of time before one of 'em stumbles onto us."

Behind them, Matthew drenched the fire with a bucket of water and spread a soiled and blackened buckskin over the wet ashes to keep the smoke from escaping. They kept the fire burning each day long enough to roast a few thin strips of venison and brew enough tea to last the three of them until the following morning. It had become monotonous fare.

Cub caught a slight movement out of the corner of one eye. He turned his head and studied the heavily wooded area in front of their campsite. He hissed and pointed to the southeast. A line of mounted men could be seen moving along the crest of a low, rolling hill no more than a quarter of a mile away. Behind them, several pack animals followed on rope halters. Their packs were bulging with hides.

Thomas wet his finger and held it up to test the wind. Satisfied it was blowing from the east, he breathed a sigh of relief, confident the passing Cherokees would not be able to smell their smoke. He crouched behind a large boulder as he watched the group of hunters trudge away towards the north. Under the overhang behind him, Cub and Matthew held their hands over the muzzles of the horses to prevent them from whinnying a greeting if they caught the smell of the passing horses.

"Where you reckon they're headin'?" Cub whispered to him after the Indians had disappeared into the forest.

"Over past the falls, I would guess. To Tugaloo, on the river." Thomas said.

"How far is that?"

"Ten, maybe fifteen miles." Thomas pulled off his hat and wiped a line of sweat from his forehead. "Whew! That was a near thing. I thought there weren't any trails within two miles of here." He plopped his hat back onto his head, stepped from beneath the overhang, and craned his neck to look upward at the rocky slope of the mountain. "You two stay put," he said without looking down. "I'm going to climb up a ways and have a look around. See if I can spot anything."

* * * *

That evening, Thomas sat at the front of the overhang. Other than the passing party of hunters, they had seen nothing for the rest of the day. Even so, he had been nursing an uneasy feeling all day. The appearance of the hunters could have been just chance, and they may have escaped unnoticed, but

261

what if they had been spotted? He voiced his opinions to the others.

"That's always a chance," Cub told him. "If you think we need to get, we'll light out right now. No sense waitin' 'til mornin'. If they spotted us, they'll come howling down on us at first light."

Thomas shook his head. "Something keeps naggin' at the back of my head, sayin' go, but I can't bring myself to do it. What if we ride out tonight and Lynn Celia comes in tomorrow with those two Muscogees?" He looked towards his brother who sat to one side, his back propped against a saddle, half asleep. "Matthew, what do you say?"

"The smart thing is to go," Matthew muttered without opening his eyes. "But I'll do as you say."

Thomas looked towards Cub. "Matthew's all by himself. You have a wife and young'uns to worry about."

Cub rubbed his chin as he thought, remaining silent as he studied the dark outline of chestnuts, oaks, and maples that hemmed in their small camp.

"Damn! I wish Martin was here." Thomas spoke the thought aloud. "He'd know which way to jump."

Cub gave a half-smile and said, "What do you think he'd say?"

"He'd say go."

"That's just what we ought to do. If we stay and get caught, we're dead. If we go, and them Muscogees show up with Lynn Celia, they'll just head on down to Augusta with her." He spread his hands. "I don't want to give advice you'll hold against me later, but you know as well as I do Martin would say 'go'. There was at least ten Cherokees in that party this mornin'. Common sense says at least one of them noticed something. They ain't as dumb as those army officers seem to think they are."

"Damn!" Thomas spoke through clenched teeth. "It's a hard thing." He fell silent, pondering his options.

"You two notice anything?" Matthew said, still without opening his eyes.

"What?" Thomas said. "You hear something?"

"I don't hear a thing. That's what I was askin' after."

For the first time, Thomas noticed the absence of insect sounds in the night. Not a cricket chirped, not a katydid voiced its perpetual argument as to whether Katy did, or didn't do *whatever it was she was supposed to do*. Far off, the mournful hoot of an owl called in the darkness. Almost immediately it was answered. Thomas felt his throat tighten.

"Saddle up," he said, and grabbed his musket.

* * * *

The Cherokees materialized from out of the night. Ten of them stood in a semi-circle outside the overhang. They appeared as dark outlines in the silvery glow of a cloudless night. Most of them held muskets, one or two were armed with French-made tomahawks; all were painted for war. The leader of the group pointed to one of the warriors and motioned him forward. The man moved forward and knelt by the ashes of the fire. Holding his hand over the ashes, he found them cold.

He moused about the trampled area under the overhang, examining the horse droppings and running his hands across the tracks in the sand. Satisfied, he pointed to the south and spoke in Cherokee.

The warriors turned and trotted into the night.

* * * *

Thomas held up his hand as a signal to the others and reined in his mount on the bank of a small stream. He estimated they had ridden at least fifteen miles since scurrying from the camp last night. To the east, the sun was inching above the horizon, the air was icy cold, with flecks of sleet blowing in from the north. The frozen breath of both riders and horses swirled in the air as the three men eyed the frigid, gray water flowing along the shallow stream bed at their feet. There was a thin layer of ice along both banks. Using skills learned from Martin, Thomas led the other men into the water and rode upstream for over a mile before leaving the water and circling in a wide arc that led them back to their original trail. An hour later, he paused at the base of a low hill and handed his reins to Matthew.

"I'm gonna have a look-see over this hill," he said. "If I remember right, we passed by it on the way south." He blew on his fingers to warm them and nodded to indicate an ancient oak with a large canopy of bare, spreading branches that drooped towards the ground. "Tie the horses under that tree," he said. "Dry their legs and rub 'em down real good to warm 'em up. When you're done, get some shuteye. If anyone's followin', they'll pass on the other side of that hill over yonder." He pointed through the trees to a small wooded rise sloping upward to the east. "By the time they find where we've circled back, we'll be two or three hours ahead of 'em." He gave them a wiry grin.

"I'll watch from up there for an hour, then wake one of you to take a turn."

Thomas crept to the top of the hill where he wedged himself among a cluster of boulders. From there, he had a clear view of the trail below. He lay his musket across his lap and leaned against one of the boulders as he kept watch for their pursuers. The country was crowded with tall underbrush on the rolling hills, a good area for moving on horseback. He calculated their chances of escaping were pretty good.

One hour later, Thomas shook Cub awake. Without exchanging words the two men swapped places. Thomas was asleep almost as soon as his head touched the rolled blanket Cub had been using as a pillow. He awoke to a gentle nudge against his side.

He looked up at Matthew, who knelt at his side with his arms crossed and both hands tucked under his armpits. Matthew's teeth chattered with a faint tapping sound. "That Cherokee war party just passed by not five minutes ago. I waited 'til I was sure they were well past us before takin' a chance on leaving my cover up there." He jerked his head in the direction of the hill.

Thomas rubbed his eyes. "How many?" he asked through a huge yawn.

"Ten. Four were mounted, the rest were afoot. They're movin' slow. If we head east right now, they'll never catch us." He raised his eyebrows and shrugged his shoulders. "Unless they know this trick. If so, they'll send back their mounted men to check on us while the others ferret out our trail at the creek."

Thomas yawned again and nodded. He reached out and prodded Cub awake.

* * * *

The three men led their mounts up the hill, frozen dew and ice-caked forest debris crunching beneath their feet. Squatting just below the crest, they paused for one last look before showing themselves on the far side. Their heads shifted back and forth, attempting to capture even the slightest hint of danger. Both Cub and Matthew looked towards Thomas, who sniffed the air like a bloodhound as he came to some inner conclusion. He motioned them down the hill. At the bottom, he paused to listen. A slight sound caught his attention. He spun to face north and crouched in the middle of the trail, musket held at the ready. "Damn!" he hissed, as two riders popped into view less than a hundred yards away.

Loving Lynn Celia

CHAPTER TWENTY-THREE

In Cherokee Country
January 21, 1761

"Wait!" Thomas cried. He reached out and pushed the barrel of Matthew's musket off target just in time to prevent him from firing. At the same time, he waved his free hand in Cub's direction, motioning for him to hold his fire. "Those are our men comin' back."

The two Muscogees lowered their weapons and walked their mounts forward. They spoke quickly to Thomas, who answered them with a mixture of their own language and signs. Their meaning was clear as they pointed to the south, warning of the little time they had before the Cherokees appeared. This was an old trick they reminded him, it wouldn't take the Cherokees long to figure it out.

The five men rode to the northeast at a canter, unmindful of the noise made by their passing. Any pursuit would be far behind. The few mounted Cherokees among those trailing them would be in no hurry to overtake them now that the two Muscogees had joined them. Their pursuers would follow cautiously, waiting to catch them when their guard was down.

Loving Lynn Celia

* * * *

After crossing the Savannah River, they stopped to rest their mounts on the east bank. The two Muscogees knelt alongside Thomas on a small spit of sand at the river's edge. With the point of his scalping knife, one of them drew a crude map on the ground, pointing out the villages and trails they had traveled in their search for Lynn Celia. Shaking their heads, they both admitted they thought she was most likely dead. They had ridden as far north as Watauga, they said, without finding any trace of her. There, a large group of Cherokees had robbed them of the trade goods and warned them away after giving them the scalp of a dark-haired Englishwoman. The Muscogee slid his knife back into its scabbard and stood. Grim-faced, he lifted the flap of a beaded pouch and produced the scalp. He held it out to Thomas. Its long, dark tresses had been combed and oiled, the inside of the skin had been dyed and contained a series of pictographs detailing the history of the trophy. The warrior shrugged. There was no way of knowing if this was, in fact, Lynn Celia's scalp. But, he said, even if she were still alive, the Cherokees were in no mood to talk with any Englishman, much less release one of their captives.

The warrior lay the scalp in Thomas's hand. Thomas's head shot back as if he had been struck in the forehead and his knees buckled. In a daze, he wobbled to a nearby tree and collapsed against its trunk. He howled in anguish, unmindful of the dangers stalking them. When they headed south a few hours later, Cub and Matthew had to wrestle him into his saddle and lead his horse while he rocked lethargically along, oblivious to everything but his own sorrow.

Satisfied they had fulfilled their agreement, the two Muscogees watched the three white men ride away before they turned their mounts, re-crossed the river, and headed for home. They knew they would be safe. The Cherokees would not risk starting a war with the Creek Confederacy by harming them. The three white men were a different matter. If they were caught, the treatment they could expect would be both harsh and painful.

That evening, the three men camped in an abandoned cabin forty miles north of Ninety-Six. The logs of the cabin showed definite signs of a recent struggle. While Thomas listlessly kindled a fire, Matthew and Cub pried distorted musket balls from the outside walls with the tip of their hunting knives.

"I wonder where the people got off to?" Cub thought aloud.

"You don't think they was taken?" Matthew asked.

Cub shook his head and continued to pick lead from the logs. "If they hadn't beaten off the attack, the cabin would be burned. I would bet they escaped—at least from here." He turned and scanned the woods bordering the small clearing. "Whether or not they survived after that..." He made a small motion with one hand, the meaning was clear.

"You think it's all right if I hunt up some fresh meat?" Matthew said. He slid his hunting knife back into its sheath and pocketed a handful of deformed musket balls he would mold into fresh ammunition later.

Cub grimaced, unsure of their safety. Still, the thought of fresh meat after living on nothing but jerky and stale cornbread for two weeks was tempting. He peered through the doorway at Thomas. He was sitting cross-legged by the makings of a fire with his head bowed and his face cradled in both hands. Cub turned away. After struggling against his inner voice counseling caution, he gave into the temptation. He nodded to Matthew. "Go ahead, but keep an eye out for danger. There's no tellin' who may hear your shot."

* * * *

Someone did hear the shot. Matthew returned at sundown, flanked by a detachment of Rangers wearing the uniform of the South Carolina Provincial Regiment, blue coats with red cuffs and facings. All six wore a leather cap with an upturned brim. The crescent moon, symbol of South Carolina, was affixed to its center.

Leading the group was an old acquaintance of Thomas and Cub, Sergeant Sanders. Martin Grubb and Winslow Driggers rode at his side. The men had been patrolling the area to the west, hoping to intercept any war parties moving up or down the Savannah River.

"What fool told *this* fool to go huntin'?" The sergeant declared gruffly. He jerked a thumb in Matthew's direction. "Damned Cub, I thought we'd taught you better than that!" He went on, letting it be known in no uncertain terms that he was not impressed by Cub's decision. He turned a jaundiced eye on Martin. "Who taught this upstart about livin' in Indian country?"

Martin rolled his eyes and looked away, pretending to find something of great interest in a nearby cedar tree.

"I guess it wasn't smart, come to think of it." Cub looked down and ran the toe of his shoe across the loose sand like a boy standing before a displeased school master.

Sanders lay back his head and bellowed. "At least you know you've been a fool! Most men would stand there and argue 'bout it." He let out a quick huff. "Well, since we can't take back the sound of that musket, we may as well eat this venison." He pointed to two of the men who rode at the rear of the small detachment. "You two get us some poles so's we can rig up a spit to turn this on." He cut his eyes towards Thomas, who stood in the doorway of the cabin. "You can tell us how the three of you came to be here while we eat."

Thomas nodded, his face a mask of anguish. The sergeant gave him a hesitant look and opened his mouth to speak, thought better of it, and instead, cleared his throat. He waved Matthew forward, a yearling doe, skinned and field dressed, was draped over his saddle.

"This ought to feed us," Cub said. "How many men do you have, sergeant?"

"Ten, eleven countin' myself." He made a motion northward with one hand. "I sent five of them out that-a-way to make sure those Cherokees this fella told us about wasn't anywhere near." He indicated Matthew with a bob of his head. "We may just ride out that direction in the morning and set an ambush, just in case they're still followin'." He grinned in Cub's direction. "Want to come along?"

Cub laughed. "I'm no soldier any more. Ain't that what they pay you fellas for?" Cub reached out and felt the fabric of the sergeant's coattail. "When did you decide to join the regulars?"

"Just as soon as I found out I was out of money and there wasn't any other way to get it."

"Whatever they're payin' you, it's too much." Cub laughed at his own joke. Several of the Rangers directed malevolent stares in his direction. Cub ignored them.

"Just like a damned civilian!" Sanders barked. "Always complaining about the pay we get, then wantin' us to risk gettin' killed chasin' Indians for them. It's enough to make a man feel unappreciated."

Cub grinned at the old soldier. "Put your horses over on the picket line and light awhile. We'll all eat good in a few hours."

Loving Lynn Celia

* * * *

Thomas sat inside the cramped cabin, staring into the fire, and barely listening as the Rangers swapped stories with Matthew and Cub. He took no part in the conversation, scarcely looking up while Martin told of several skirmishes he'd been in since leaving Savannah. He displayed a handful of scalps as proof. "That's over four hundred Pounds Sterling your lookin' at!" he bragged. "If I can ever get them to North Carolina to cash 'em in."

Winslow Driggers dismissed Martin's boast with a wave of his hand. "Don't stop breathin' while you're a waitin' on them North Carolina folks to pay for those South Carolina scalps. It'll be a cold day in hell 'fore you see any of that money."

"A scalp's a scalp. Ain't no way for folks to tell where they came from. 'Sides, every Cherokee kilt in South Carolina is one less to raise hell in North Carolina. Seems to me they ought to be grateful to me for helpin' 'em out." Martin bobbed his head, satisfied he had proved the veracity of his argument.

"You two boys ought to be married the way you carry on," Sanders complained. "Why don't the two of you hold your tongues for a while and let these folks tell how they came to be here."

Thomas thought for a moment. "I don't rightly know where to start."

"From the beginning is the best place," Sanders said.

Thomas told his story, ending with the conclusion of the two Muscogees, that Lynn Celia was dead.

"Sons-of-bitches," one of the men muttered under his breath.

Thomas pretended not to hear him.

"I'm mortal sorry to hear that, Thomas," Sergeant Sanders said. He looked down and studied the earthen floor of the cabin. When he looked up, he peered at Cub for a moment and shook his head. One corner of his lips turned upward in a sad smile. "Be that as it may. You three must have the luck of the Irish in you. This whole area is swarming with Cherokees on the lookout for stragglers just like you. It's a small miracle you made it as far as you did without runnin' into some of them." He leaned back against the log wall behind him and rubbed his full stomach. "We're no more than ten miles from the old Cherokee town of Seneca. Their war parties still use it as a rendezvous goin' to and from the settlements. You best stay with us 'til we get back to Fort Prince George. I can't spare any men for an escort, we're almost too small a band as it is. And travelin' by yourselves down to Ninety-Six or Augusta? Why, you're almost sure to run onto a war party before you get there."

"When's the last time you fellas had a run in with them?" Cub asked.

"Two days ago. We had a brush with a small party, wounded one or two before they got away. The week before, we came across what was left of a family about five miles north of here." He looked around the small cabin. "Could have been these people."

All eyes turned, peering through the open door of the cabin. Outside, it had begun to snow. The light of the half-moon, reflecting from the thin blanket of white, illuminated the night with a cool, silvery glow. One of the sentries hurried in from his post at the edge of the woods. His boots creating a series of steady crunching sounds. Ice crystals, formed from his frozen breath, left a wispy trail behind him as he made his way across the small clearing. He paused just outside the door. "Someone's comin'," he said through the opening.

G.G. Stokes, Jr.

The Rangers lunged for their weapons. With practiced skill they smothered the fire and took up defensive positions around the inside of the cabin. They used doors and windows where possible. In places where there were no openings, they dug the chinking from between the logs with the points of their bayonets to create loopholes to fire from. To the north, they could see the shadowy forms of riders, black outlines against the whiteness of the earth, fluttering between the tree trunks. And they were drawing closer.

Loving Lynn Celia

CHAPTER TWENTY-FOUR

In Cherokee Country
January 21, 1761

Sergeant Sanders lowered his rifle. "It's our boys comin' back in," he said over his shoulder. Around the cabin, Thomas heard the clamor of locks being set to half-cock. One of the men stirred the ashes of the fire with a stick and threw a handful of kindling over the red coals.

The riders stopped at the edge of the clearing and conferred with one of the sentries before dismounting and walking their mounts to the picket line. Their leader detached himself from the group and drifted towards the cabin. He nodded in Sander's direction,

"Got anything hot to eat or drink?"

The five men, half frozen, dusted snow from their uniforms and crouched in a ring about the fire as they ate. John Ozborne, the leader of the small group, made his report through gulps of hot tea and bites of half-cooked venison.

"We found the group of warriors followin' these folks," Ozborne said, jerking his head in the direction of Thomas and Cub. "We watched 'em for a while once they cut our trail. They were mighty skittish acting. 'Bout two hours ago, a second group came in from the east." He looked towards Sanders, swallowed, and said, "Didn't know we was bein' followed too, did you?"

"Damn!" Sanders said. "How many?"

"I counted twenty-three." He inclined his head towards Thomas and Cub once again. "Plus the ten chasin' them. That makes thirty-three to our fourteen."

He smiled, displaying a checkerboard of missing teeth. Those still remaining were darkly stained by tobacco. "All well-armed, too. At least those followin' us. Each of them carryin' a musket. I saw one or two with rifles."

Sanders nodded. "Well, one thing's for sure, if we light out now, they'll be able to catch us in no time. A blind man can follow our trail in the snow, even at night. Did you get the feelin' they know where we are?"

Ozborne shrugged. "They probably know about this place. More'n likely they're the ones that attacked it."

Sanders rolled his eyes and tapped his lips with his fingers while he thought. He looked towards Martin and Winslow. "What do you two think? If we stay here, we won't leave any tracks. Maybe they'll think we kept on goin' before the snow came on." Martin shrugged. "They may find us if we stay put. On the other hand, if we move in this snow, they'll catch us for sure."

Winslow rubbed his fingers across the stubble on his chin. "I think they'll find us either way. But here, at least, we'll have cover. Out there? If they catch us in the open it'll go hard on us." He looked towards the other man who had turned back to the fire and was holding his hands, palms out, to its warmth. Ozborne craned his neck in Winslow's direction without moving his hands from the small circle of warmth radiated by the flames. "You think the snow'll cover your tracks by morning?" Winslow asked.

"Hell, if it keeps up like this, it'll cover them in a few hours."

Winslow nodded. "I guess that's it. Let's stay put and hope they just ride on by."

Sergeant Sanders agreed. He pointed out three men. "You relieve the sentries out there. I'll send someone out to take your place in a couple of hours." He looked around the room at the other men, studying their faces in the flickering firelight. "The rest of you get some sleep. It's goin' to be a long day tomorrow."

Groans, and snores, and coughs were soon mingled with the crackling of the fire. Thomas lit the taper in a battered candle lantern left behind when the cabin's owners had fled. Using its dull glow, he studied the scalp the Muscogee had given him, running the strands of hair through his fingers and holding it up to the light to study small imperfections. "This isn't my wife's hair."

Sanders, who was dozing at his side, woke with a start. With a sigh, he pushed himself to a sitting position and rubbed the sleep from his eyes. "What was that, Thomas?"

"This isn't my wife's hair," Thomas repeated. "Look here." He pushed the long tresses towards the sergeant. "It doesn't feel right. Lynn Celia's hair was as fine as a baby's. This is coarse. Run your fingers through it."

Sanders hesitated for a moment. He reached out and rubbed a lock of the hair between his thumb and forefinger. "It is pretty stiff," he said.

"Yes." Thomas spoke the word to himself, nodding as he did so. "And look here," he went on, "there's two or three gray hairs in the front. They're hard to see, but you can make them out." He feathered the strands and pointed them out. "Lynn Celia didn't have a gray hair on her head. It can't be hers."

"She'd been through a lot," Sanders said. He knew from experience that grief-stricken people would grasp at the slightest straw, searching for one glimmer of hope. "And with bear grease rubbed into it, well, it would make anything feel coarser and thicker than it really is."

Thomas shook his head. "No," he said. "I know my wife. I've brushed her hair a hundred times." He turned to stare into the fire. A faraway look crept into his face as he remembered happier times. Memories of nights spent sitting with her in front of their own hearth, with the children asleep and their Saturday baths done. He felt a tear form at the corner of one eye and dribble down his cheek as the bittersweet memories of those days overwhelmed him. He remembered the sweet smell of the honeysuckle Lynn Celia would brush through her hair in the summer, the smoothness of her shoulders. He took a deep breath. "This isn't hers. She's still alive."

Sanders nodded. If the thought that there was still a chance of seeing his wife again helped to ease the sorrow for a few weeks or months, what would it hurt? He held out his hand. "If you're certain it's not hers, let me have it." Thomas hesitated, studying the hair for a moment longer before handing it over.

Taking the scalp, Sanders folded the skin side outward and showed the markings to Thomas.

"See these marks?" he said. "They tell the story of this woman." He paused and tossed a pebble at Martin. The sleeping man sat up with a start, instantly awake.

"Come over here and read these markings for us, Martin," Sanders said, shaking the scalp in the other man's direction.

Martin rose and stepped across two sleeping forms huddled with their feet to the fire. He flopped down alongside Thomas. "Here," he said, and reached for the scalp.

Wrapping the hair around his hand so that the painted skin showed, he held it up to the light. He ran his finger across the markings on the skin. "This large blue hoop, means it's the scalp of a grown woman," he said. He pulled the skin away to expose the wood beneath it. "The skin's painted yellow with red tears. It means she was a mother. The strange thing about this is the hair's not braided. If it was, it would mean she was a wife." He studied the markings for a moment, mumbled "Strange," to himself. "This black circle, all the way around the outside of the skin, signifies she died at night, and the black knife, well, that's clear, she was either stabbed to death or had her throat cut." He pointed to a small red mark that resembled a small foot. "See this? It means she died fighting.

Put it all together and we have a woman living alone, most likely a widow, with children. She was killed by a knife at night, and went down fightin', defending her young'uns." He unrolled the scalp and combed the long tresses with his fingers. "I'd say thirty to thirty-five years old."

"You can tell all of that just by lookin' at these signs?" Thomas asked in amazement.

Martin nodded. "Up north of here, the Injuns make a livin' off scalps. They use those markings so that when they sell 'em, they can get paid top price." "From the French?"

"I guess. But the British buy them, too."

Thomas glanced at the scalp. "It's not Lynn Celia's hair, is it?"

Martin shook his head, "No, it ain't," he said. He made a move to throw it into the fire.

"Wait!" Sanders barked. "If it don't belong to Thomas's wife, we need to find out who it belongs to. Someone loved her. Maybe we can find out who."

"Anyone who loved this woman died with her," Martin said. He shrugged and held the scalp out to the sergeant.

---

1 The information about the marking of scalps, is from Allen W. Eckert's, "Wilderness War", Bantam books, Pg. 523

Loving Lynn Celia

CHAPTER TWENTY-FIVE

Augusta, Georgia
May 8, 1761

Thomas handed his hammer to his son, Richard. He wiped the sweat from his brow with the sleeve of his work shirt and tousled his son's hair. "What do you want for your birthday when me and grandpa get back from Savannah?" he asked the soon-to-be four-year-old.

Richard looked up and smiled. "A musket!" he announced proudly.

"A musket?" Thomas was surprised by the request. "Why do you want a musket?"

Richard blew out his small chest and seemed to swell with pride. "I want a musket so's I can go and get my mama back from those thievin' Injuns up there." He pointed upriver.

Roger Claxton, now a strapping, snaggle-toothed, five-year-old, sat on top of the flatboat's cabin sorting through a pile of cedar shingles that would be used to repair leaks on the roof before the boat's downriver journey began. He rolled his eyes at the innocent simplicity of his half-brother. "You couldn't even hold a musket up, much less shoot it," he said with a wave of his hand meant to shoo away such a silly idea.

"I could too!" Richard wailed. He rolled his eyes upward at his father. "Couldn't I, pa?"

With a smile, Thomas plucked the chubby-faced child from the deck of the flatboat and plopped him onto the roof of the cabin, alongside Roger. "I'm sure you could," he said. "If it was shortened a bit, like those the Rangers use."

The eyes of both boy's flared with excitement at the mention of their heroes, the troop of Georgia Rangers operating in and around Augusta. The Rangers were, for all practical purposes, the law in this part of the colony. Their duties included everything from repelling invasion by hostile Indians to serving warrants issued by the royal authorities in Savannah.

Thomas's great-uncle, Morgan, was a lieutenant in the Rangers and the two boys never tired of sitting alongside him during his visits to their grandparent's home. They were fascinated by the wooden peg that served as his right leg. "I want me one of them wooden legs," Roger declared. "Uncle Morgan says his toes never get cold, and if a rattler strikes, it don't hurt a bit! Why I bet he could walk through a whole pit of rattlers without gettin' hurt."

Richard giggled and kicked his feet against the side of the cabin. He held out his arms. "Put me down pa," he said. He found it hard to sit still for long.

Thomas sat both boys on the deck and shooed them towards the shore. "You two run along now," he said. "Time to get over to Mrs. Paxton's and learn your letters." "Why do we have to learn letters?" Roger wanted to know.

"You don't read, and you can do anything worth doin'." Richard added. Roger nodded in agreement. Both boys were certain they had a convincing argument.

Thomas drew himself erect and, with hands on hips, glared down at the two miscreants. "What will your mama say when she comes home?" He scowled. "She would be sorely disappointed in you—and me, if she came home to find the two of you couldn't read like her. Why, once these Indian troubles are cleared up, and your ma's back, this country will fill up like it is around Savannah. A man who can't read and write won't have a chance."

"What about you, pa?" Roger asked. He seemed troubled by the idea of his father being left out.

"Me?" Thomas pointed to his chest with his thumb. "Well, I'll have the two of you to look out

291

for me. And your sister too, once she's old enough."

"Ok, Pa," Richard said. Slump-shouldered with despair, the two turned to go, saw the gangplank leading to the shore, and raced for it, each determined to be the first across.

"Be careful!" Thomas shouted at their backs. He cringed in anticipation of seeing one or both of them fall into the mud along the riverbank. In the blink of an eye, both stood clean and dry on the bank, waving over their shoulders as they plodded towards the town. They both squealed with delight as their grandfather Richard rumbled past in a wagon loaded with skins. The older man shouted a greeting and tossed a piece of homemade candy to each of them.

Two of the flatboat's crewmen rode in the bed of the wagon along with the load. They jumped to the ground as soon as the cart came to a stop.

"We'll start loadin' today," Richard said. "That'll mean two of us will have to stay on the boat each night as guards." He indicated the two men lugging a bale of furs with a slight movement of his hand. "These two are stayin' tonight. We'll stay tomorrow."

After lashing the bundles to the deck and covering them with canvas, Thomas and his father headed for home. Egrain, whose name had slowly evolved to Grainy over the years, ran out to meet them. She jumped into Thomas' arms. "Hello, birthday girl!"

Thomas grinned. "Just how old are you today?"

Grainy held up three fingers, giggled, and nuzzled her face into the nape of his neck to hide her embarrassment.

"Three!" Thomas declared in mock surprise. "Why I can't believe you're only three. As big as you are? Grandma says she could never get along without your help. Surely, you must be at least … four?"

"Daddy!" Grainy cried. She poked out her lower lip, pouting. "Grandma says you have a present for me."

"I do, but you can't have it 'til noon."

Grainy bounced in his arms. "Daddy!" she cried again. Her face twisted upward with an impatient and wanting expression. "Not 'til noon?"

"Not 'til noon," Thomas repeated. He sat her on the ground and gave her tiny bottom an affectionate pat. "Run along, now," he said. "And help grandma get the food ready.

The quicker we eat, the quicker you get your present."

Loving Lynn Celia

He smiled as the three-year-old, loose blonde hair trailing in the wind, scurried across the bare earth of the cabin's yard. When she disappeared into the lean-to used as a communal kitchen for the extended family, his face clouded. *How I wish her mother could be here to see her grow,* he thought.

* * * *

"Well, Thomas," Susannah, his sister, said. "I think you've kept Grainy waitin' quite long enough for her present." She fingered the new mobcap on Grainy's head, a present from the child's grandmother. "My, don't you look like a grown woman, it's almost a sin to cover that beautiful blond hair. Like as not, it'll grow dark by the time you're old enough to wed." Grainy's eyes glowed in response to the praise. She looked towards her father, certain he was the bearer of some strange and wonderful gift.

"Don't you want to finish eating first?" Thomas teased. Taking his hunting bag from a peg by the door, he pulled a wooden box from it and set it on the table in front of the wide-eyed child with a flourish. "Go ahead, open it," he said with a smile.

Grainy's two brothers all but crushed her between themselves as they crowded around for a closer look. Across the table, Patience fidgeted with the hem of her apron. Her own birthday had been exactly one month ago when she had turned thirteen.

Grainy reached in, lifting a small, linen-wrapped article from the box. Giddy with excitement, she unwrapped the small silver comb and held it up for everyone to see. The women in the room were stricken silent, the brothers hissed, they had been hoping for a kite. What good was a comb? They wanted to know.

"Why land's sake, Thomas!" Susannah said. "That's a right expensive present for a three-year-old."

"What of it?" Thomas answered in a haughty voice. "It'll last her all her life."

Grainy bounded from her chair and bounced into her father's lap. She curled up, resting her head against his chest, her every feature glowing with happiness.

* * * *

That evening, Thomas and his father sat side by side in front of a low fire, rocking slowly, and puffing on long clay pipes. His mother sat in one corner, away from the heat, her knitting needles clicking as she worked in the dim light of a candle lantern. In the loft, Grainy and Patience sat cross-legged. Grainy sat in front, her head held at an angle and her eyes closed as Patience ran the silver comb through her long, silky tresses. Roger and little Richard sat to one side of the hearth, shaving small slivers from a piece of seasoned apple wood and tossing them into the flames. They watched, fascinated, as the tiny coils of wood burst into rainbows of colored flames.

"You reckon we'll be finished loading tomorrow?" Thomas said without taking his eyes from the fire. He seemed as mesmerized by the colorful flames as the two boys.

Richard nodded. "We'll set off for Savannah the day after tomorrow." He took a long draught from his pipe and held it in, savoring the flavor. He smiled and blew the smoke through his nose. "It's a wonder we have as many skins as we do, what with this war and all that's happenin' up north."

Thomas opened his mouth to speak, shut it, and turned to look towards the door of the cabin. He could hear the sounds of approaching riders. One of the dogs began a furious barking, others came running from the nearby cabins to join in. Thomas followed his father across the puncheon floor and stood to one side as he drew the bolt and swung the

296

door inward. Outside, his hand still cocked and ready to knock, stood Cub. In the darkness behind him, Martin Grubb sat hunched over the pommel of his saddle, his tongue working inside one cheek as he settled a fresh chaw of tobacco into place. He leaned forward to spit a long brown stream onto the head of a sad-looking hound that stood to one side, baying up at him like a treed a coon. The dog rolled to one side and began pawing at the offending mass with a hind paw.

"Evenin'," Martin said in a tired drawl. It seemed to take all of his energy to get the word to come out.

"Evenin'," Thomas answered. He thrust his hand in Cub's direction. "Good to see ya'll again," he said, as they shook hands. With the other hand he gave Cub an affectionate pat on the shoulder. "What brings the two of you all the way to Augusta?"

"We came to get you," Cub said. "You know about the army the British have sent to Charleston?"

Thomas nodded. He motioned Cub inside. "Martin, you light and come on in, it looks like you could use a rest. You'll both stay here for the night, of course," he said. He motioned for the two boys, who stood staring around their grandfather's legs, to come forward. "Roger, you and little Richard get these horses stabled. Put 'em over in your Aunt Susannah's barn. She's got plenty of room."

Martin handed Richard his reins. "Make sure you give them a good rub down and plenty of feed. There's a penny for each of you if you do a good job." He laughed as he said it and patted Richard on the head. "You've grown a good three inches since the last time I saw you," he observed. Looking at Thomas, he said, "You've been well?" "Quite." Thomas nodded. "Come on in."

Inside the cabin, Thomas's mother scurried about to get the table ready for the men. "You boys must be hungry," she said, motioning for them to take a seat on a long bench running alongside a puncheon table in the center of the room. "We've still got some *hasty pudding* warming from supper." She swung an iron pot, suspended on a crane, from the fireplace and lifted the lid, peering inside to gage whether or not there was enough left for two men. Satisfied there was, she stirred the pot's contents with a long-handled maple spoon before dipping a generous helping onto two wooden trenchers and setting one before each man. Looking up into the loft, she called for Patience to carve two slabs of meat from a cured ham hanging from the rafters. She looked towards her husband.

"Richard, you run over to the store and fetch a jug of rum." Satisfied she had done her duty, she dropped back into her rocker. The steady clicking of her knitting needles resumed.

The travelers shoveled the food into their mouths. Both were famished after their long ride. Thomas pulled a ladder-back chair up to the end of the table and sat silently, puffing on his pipe as the two men ate.

Martin finished first. He turned to eye Thomas for a moment before he spoke. "You can guess why we've come," he said. "We told you we'd come fetch you when the army was ready to move back into the Cherokee country."

In the corner, the clicking of Lucretia's knitting needles came to an abrupt halt. "They fixin' to move?"

"Yes ma'am. They'll be marchin' in a few days if they ain't already started."

"How many?" Thomas asked.

"Between two and three thousand, they say. We've been transferred to one of the new companies." Martin inclined his head to indicate Cub. "He joined up, too. We figured on you comin' along. Sergeant Sanders sent us out. He wants us to find as many of the men who marched with Montgomerie as we can and talk them into joining

299

up. We need at least twenty-five more men to get the company up to strength for this campaign."

Thomas nodded. "You know I'll be goin'. But it'll only be on the condition that if I find any trace of Lynn Celia, I'll be free to go after her."

Martin nodded. "Sanders knows that, Cub here said the same thing. And I'll damned sure be with you." He stopped and took a gulp of water from a wooden noggin. "I wish your father would hurry back with the rum," he muttered to himself. "I would just about say the whole damned company will go with you if there's a chance to get her back." He checked himself and turned towards Lucretia. "Sorry ma'am," he said to her. "I been around soldiers too long. A man tends to forget his manners."

CHAPTER TWENTY-SIX

Fort Prince George, South Carolina
May 29, 1761

Thomas stood on the ramparts of Fort Prince George, cheering and waving his hat in welcome as the first lines of Colonel Grant's scarlet-clad regulars emerged from the dark line of forest to the south.

He had been in the fort a week, waiting for this moment—the moment that signaled the start of the expedition intended to break, once and for all, the power of the Cherokee nation. Cub and Martin stood beside him, along with Sergeant Sanders, Winslow Driggers and Christopher Christ. All of them were looking forward to the adventure on which they were about to embark, Martin, more so than the others. The value of his scalp collection had grown to over seven hundred pounds in the past few months, and he was certain, with luck, he would end this campaign with at least a thousand pounds in cash money.

In his hand, Thomas held the newest product of Christopher Christ's skills, a fifty-four-caliber rifle. He had used what savings he had to purchase the rifle. With its brass barrel bands and ornate brass patch box, it was a fancier piece than Thomas had planned on buying, but it could place a ball in a six-inch circle at one hundred yards and it weighed a good three pounds less than his old musket. Still, he had kept his old doglock, knowing it would be more useful in the close, hand-to-hand fighting they would encounter once they rode into the hostile mountains that frowned down on them from the northwest.

Rank after rank of soldiers came into view as the army moved into the open. Tramping towards the ford, and marching to the cadence of drums and pipes, they followed the road skirting the river. There, they halted. The voices of officers and sergeants floated across the open ground as they yelped commands at the stationary files of men. The entire line seemed to fly apart like a covey of quail. In a few hours, the open area around the fort was filled with rows of canvas tents and with the wispy gray smoke of cooking fires. A herd of several hundred cattle grazed between the fort and the river. Picket lines containing hundreds of horses stretched into the distance. To the backwoods men watching from the fort, it looked as if the whole world had descended on the Cherokee nation.

G.G. Stokes, Jr.

"Well, I reckon this'll finish off the Cherokees," Winslow Driggers drawled. He leaned forward and spit a stream of tobacco juice over the top of the wall. "At least if they listen to us provincials." He wiped the corner of his mouth with the back of one hand and transferred the stain to the outside of his breeches leg. "When it comes to Indian fightin', we could show those regulars a thing or two."

"I've heard this Colonel Grant gets along well with our officers," Sergeant Sanders remarked. He motioned to Thomas and Martin. "You two come with me, I want to talk to those South Carolina troops down there. See what news they're bringin' with 'em."

The provincial's camp proved to be a confusion of sights, sounds, and smells. Weapons and gear were strewn about haphazardly in small piles that belonged to individual soldiers or militia units. The tents the militia had been forced to use because of the rainy weather were pitched at odd angles, clustered together in small knots. Some of the officers had attempted to lay out their camps in some semblance of military order, but it was clear herding cats would have been easier than making militiamen act like regulars. The one exception was the camp of the South Carolina Provincial Regiment. The men, dressed in their neat blue uniforms, seemed more inclined to discipline than their comrades who milled about in homespun and linen.

Sergeant Sanders called greetings to several old friends as three men approached the bivouac. One well-dressed man smiled and threw up his hand in welcome as he recognized Sanders. "Well I'll be," the man called, "the Cherokees ain't got you, yet?" His smile broadened. "Come on over and have a seat, we're just fixin' to eat." He indicated a large rock with a gallant sweep of one hand. "Sorry we can't offer you more, but all we have is cornmeal. We've been mixing it into dough and using our ramrods to bake it over the coals. You're welcome to all you can eat."

"I think I'll wait 'til they slaughter a few of those cattle," Sanders said. He backed up to the rock and rested his buttocks against it.

"Wait if you want to," the man threw the words over one shoulder as he turned his ramrod over the fire. "Myself, I'm ready to eat right now."

"Any news from the low country?" Sanders asked. He canted his rifle against the rock and folded his arms.

"Not much, everybody's talking about you fellas up here. We was kinda hopin' you'd have the war won by the time we got here." He lay the dough wrapped ramrod aside to cool and sat on a folding campstool, looking up at Sanders. "We've got somewhere around twenty-five hundred men. Regulars, Rangers and provincials. Quite a few came down from North Carolina when they heard Middleton was getting' up a regiment of his own. We're with Colonel Waddell," he said. He made a slight movement with his head to indicate the men clustered around the campfire. "He's got us divided into five companies of one hundred men each."

Sanders whistled. "What I could have done with five hundred men," he said. "How long are you mustered for?"

"Seven months. The governor reckons it'll be over by then. I sure hope so. I don't look forward to moving through those mountains in the winter."

"If Grant knows what he's doin', this should be over in a few months. Burn the towns, destroy the fields and livestock, and let nature take its course. By spring, half of 'em will have starved to death."

Thomas felt a cold lump in his stomach as he visualized Lynn Celia starving in those cold mountains along with her captors.

The man gave Thomas an odd look. "I guess that's one way of doin' it," he said. He picked up his ramrod and bit into the cornbread, stripping it from the metal like he was gnawing on an ear of corn.

A sudden hubbub of voices near the ford in the river caught the attention of the three men. Thomas nudged Sanders and jumped onto the top of the rock. He raised himself on his toes and shaded his eyes to get a better look. On the far side of the river, several Cherokees had appeared. From their dress, and the quality of their mounts, Thomas took them to be important chiefs.

Two red-coated officers mounted and splashed through the water of the ford to meet them. The officers halted just short of the four Cherokees, spoke briefly, and led the visitors into the camp. They halted outside Colonel Grant's marquee.

Word spread like a wildfire throughout the camp. Attakullakulla, one of the most important and powerful men in the Cherokee nation, had come to speak of peace. The faces of the men lifted in relief and excitement as the rumor that the war was over made its way from man to man. Everyone was sure that was the case when Colonel Grant and the small deputation of Cherokees emerged from the tent an hour later. They stood together in a tight group, chatting like old friends, shaking hands, and laughing. After exchanging a few last words, the emissaries slid onto the backs of their horses, splashed across the ford, and rode through the blackened ruins of Keowee. Thomas could see their heads move from side to side as they surveyed the devastation of the village. As they spoke among themselves, one of them paused and turned in the saddle to look back at the tents of the army that had come to destroy them. In a few short minutes they had disappeared into the high hills to the northwest.

* * * *

Colonel Grant waited seven days for the return of the Cherokee emissaries. When they failed to appear, the army marched. Trudging along rain-soaked trails, they followed Montgomerie's route of the year before, threading their way forward on the tight mountain paths and along the banks of clear, swiftly flowing streams. On the second day out of Fort Prince George, they turned to march north, up the valley leading to the middle towns. Captain Kennedy, a rough, no-nonsense officer, scoured the forest ahead of the main army. His detachment consisted of ninety Catabwas and thirty frontiersmen who were dressed and painted as Indians. The troops referred to these men as "White Indians". They glided through the forest ahead of the main army on the lookout for ambushes or spies.

Thomas and the other Rangers, along with the British light infantry, followed a half mile behind Captain Kennedy's men. To the rear of these two hundred men, the main body, consisting of over two thousand men, trudged along. Behind the main body was a long column of wagons and pack animals belonging to the supply train, and, behind them, driven along by mounted militiamen, was a large herd of cattle. A rear guard of twenty men came last, their muskets and rifles bouncing across their saddles as they rode along the rutted trail.

All in all, the army stretched out for almost two miles. On the hills and mountains that hemmed the trail in on two sides, Cherokee warriors watched and waited, biding their time until the army moved onto ground that favored them.

The evening of the third day, the invaders made camp in a large, level area just to the south of the narrow gap leading them to the first of the middle towns. Tomorrow, they would pass the site of last year's battle. Fires dotted the area. A ring of red-coated sentries secured the camp. Farther out, Rangers and Catabwas glided through the night, or lay in ambushes meant to snare any Cherokee warriors bold enough to venture near the camp.

The Catabwas and their white Indian allies were camped alongside Thomas's company of provincials. Periodically, a group of them would rise and disappear into the darkness, or return from it and roll in their blankets after gobbling down hasty meals plucked from the iron pots suspended over the glowing coals of cooking fires. For such silent and deadly foes, Thomas noticed more than a few of them were blurting out any number of sounds the human body was capable of producing.

Nursing a steaming mug of tea, Thomas leaned his back against a downed log that lay alongside his fly tent. He pulled the blanket around his shoulders and wiggled himself into the thick wool, staring into the flames of his fire. Lost in thoughts of Lynn Celia and his children, he let his mind wander. A sudden movement at the corner of his vision startled him. He jumped and reached for his musket, then relaxed as he recognized Captain Kennedy, the leader of the white Indians, approaching. Two of the Catabwas followed him.

"Howdy, Thomas," the captain threw the greeting at Thomas while he was still ten yards away.

"How do, captain," Thomas responded. "Cool night, isn't it?"

Thomas could still make out the remains of smudged paint on the captain's face when he stopped on the far side of the fire and cast an appraising look at the dark sky. "Clouds and rain always seem to send a chill into the air this time of year," the captain remarked offhandedly. He grounded his rifle and gave a slight jerk of his head in the direction of the two Catabwas. "These two Indians want to see you, but they don't speak any English. One of 'em says you done him a favor a few years back."

"Oh?" Thomas pushed the blanket from his shoulders and stood among its folds. He peered at the middle-aged warrior who stood at the captain's side. The man tossed a few guttural words in Thomas's direction. He paused and eyed Captain Kennedy while he translated them into English.

"This one's called Seven Kills," Kennedy said. He indicated the man with a slight movement of one hand. "The other's his son."

Kennedy listened with an unintentional scowl as Seven Kills began to talk. He went on for almost a full minute, the captain nodding his head every so often to indicate he was following the gist of the warrior's narrative.

When Seven Kills finished speaking, Kennedy translated. "It seems he was snake bit by your place a few years back."

Understanding flashed across Thomas's face. He snapped his fingers and smiled. "Tell him I remember," he said.

"Seven Kills says with your beard and all, he didn't recognize you when he first saw you at the fort," the captain said. He grinned and added, "Seems all white men look pretty much alike to him." He chuckled at the joke. "Anyways, he asks how your family is doin'."

Thomas shook his head. "Tell him my wife was carried off by the Cherokees last year. I haven't had a word of her since."

The captain translated and waited patiently as Seven Kills answered him, prattling on in what Thomas was certain was the story of his life. When he finished, Kennedy looked at Thomas. "What's your wife's name?"

"Lynn Celia Simpson."

The captain told the warrior, who nodded and said a few words. Kennedy turned back to face Thomas and shrugged his shoulders. "He says he'll make sure his Catabwas watch for her. If she is in any of these towns, they'll find her."

"Thank him," Thomas said. He held up his rifle. "Tell him this belongs to the man who returns her to me."

The captain translated, Seven Kills nodded somberly, and the three men turned away. Thomas watched as they moved back to their own camp where the two Catabwas rolled into their blankets. Captain Kennedy sat on a log and stared into the fire, brooding over the events of tomorrow.

G.G. Stokes, Jr.

CHAPTER TWENTY-SEVEN

Montgomerie's Battlefield
June 10, 1761

Thomas and the other provincials could smell last year's battlefield long before they could see it. As they passed along the banks of the Little Tennessee River, they glanced, grim-faced with outrage at the bones and skulls of their fellow soldiers scattered about the ground. The remains of the dead had been unearthed and rifled after the army had withdrawn. Bodies, stripped of clothing and trophies, had been left to rot on the ground. Thomas studied one skull as he passed. A few stray tendrils of hair still clung to a ring of desiccated flesh around the bald spot left when the scalp had been stripped away. Many of the bones scattered around the skull looked gnawed on; the moist morning air was heavy with the smells of mold and decay.

"Look there!" Martin exclaimed. He pointed to a skull grinning at them from atop a large rock by the trail. "I ain't hardly ever dug up a grave to get at a scalp. That's pretty low!" He felt vindicated by this discovery. Some of the troops from Charleston looked down their noses at the frontiersmen for their trafficking in scalps.

Ahead of them, a long rifle cracked, followed by silence. The men stopped and crouched protectively. Muskets and rifles, carried over the men's shoulders, were snapped downward and held at the ready. The metallic clicking of musket locks filled the air. A few men slid bayonets onto the muzzles of their weapons. A long and pregnant silence settled over the area. A twig snapped. Men jumped, startled. A few fingers jerked, almost setting off muskets or rifles when a figure sprang from the cane break ahead of them.

"Steady boys. It's Captain Kennedy," one of the officers drawled. Kennedy nodded in their direction to acknowledge them, waved them forward, turned, and disappeared back into the cane. A few men let out audible sighs of relief as they lowered their weapons.

The advance continued. As Thomas and Cub moved ahead with the front rank, Martin edged forward from the second rank to join them. "That shot alerted every Cherokee within two miles that we're comin'. Best look out for yourself." He hissed the warning to them and, without waiting

314

for a response, faded back to his place in the second line of blue-coated provincials.

The men shifted into single file as they entered the thick cane along a narrow trail.

Thomas could hear the muted voices of the men ahead as they spoke.

Cub nudged him on the back of one shoulder and pointed to the side of the trail. A dead Cherokee warrior, dressed in buckskin leggings and a blue loincloth, lay on the side of the trail. He wore a captured red coat with the regimental markings of Montgomerie's Highlanders. Both sleeves had been removed and all of the buttons were missing. There was a small round hole in the center of the man's forehead. The warrior's painted face sagged like a loose-fitting mask. His scalp and both hands were missing. Flies were already buzzing about the body by the hundreds.

"Must have been the shot we heard," Cub whispered into Thomas's back as they continued forward.

The canebrake ended as abruptly as it had begun. Within a few short steps, Thomas found himself once again in open country. Far ahead, the muted boom of a musket sounded. After a slight pause, it was answered by the sharp crack of a rifle. As if on signal, a loud wail erupted from a thousand throats

315

hidden somewhere to their right. Within seconds, it sounded like the whole world was shouting and firing muskets. Lieutenant Marion drew his sword and waved the men forward. He led them at a fast trot towards the sound of the guns.

The steady drumming of musket and rifle fire grew louder and more intense as they drew closer. Stray musketballs began to skip along the ground or thump against tree trunks. One man in Thomas's line dropped to the ground, another stumbled forward, hopping on one foot.

Captain Kennedy materialized from the thick underbrush lining the trail ahead and motioned for Lieutenant Marion to join him. The two men conferred briefly before Marion turned and ran towards the waiting men. He grabbed Sergeant Sanders by the elbow and leaned forward in order to be heard over the sound of the guns.

"Sergeant," he said, "the enemy is up ahead on a small rise to our right." He pointed with his sword in the direction of the firing. "We will form a line and advance in that direction. Tell your men as soon as we are engaged, they are to take cover and advance from tree to tree." He paused as a red-coated lieutenant from the light infantry stumbled forward. The Lieutenant was red-faced and puffing from the exertion of fighting his way through the thick cane. Lieutenant Marion briefed him while Sergeant Sanders maneuvered the provincials into two lines and shouted the order to advance.

Thomas moved forward, his rifle slung over one shoulder, advancing with his bayoneted musket against the unseen enemy. Ahead, the firing continued, the shrieks of the Cherokees increased as they threw taunts and insults into the faces of their hated enemies, the Catabwas.

Once the Rangers and provincials began advancing through the brush and trees, the Catabwas, along with Captain Kennedy's white Indians, scurried to both flanks.

"At them!" Thomas heard the command of a light infantry officer behind him. The red line, following on the heels of the provincials, surged ahead, flowing through the South Carolinians who had taken up positions behind trees and rocks and who were now firing up the hill. Lieutenant Marion's voice could be heard shouting orders and giving advice as he paced back and forth behind the lines. "Shoot high!" he warned the men, knowing most of them would undershoot when firing uphill. "Aim for the tops of their heads, or you'll be firing into the ground at their feet." He slapped the flat of his sword against the side of his leg. Thomas could tell he was *chomping at the bit* to charge that hill.

As the light infantry marched up the hill, Thomas unslung his rifle and began taking aimed shots at careless warriors who exposed themselves to snipe at the line of advancing redcoats. Behind him, the rumble of drums and the squealing of bagpipes announced the arrival of the main army. Up on the hill, the Cherokees gave way. Abandoning their positions, they retreated up the steep slope and disappeared over the crest of the hill.

Cheers erupted along the lines of provincials and light infantrymen. The cheers were short-lived as a large group of Cherokees, who had circled around behind them, opened fire from the far side of the river. Colonel Grant swung his army to face the new threat and ordered them to move forward, across the river. Thomas shook his head.

"What's wrong?" Martin called to him. His voice was barely audible above the din of battle.

"Don't you see what's happening?" he said. "This is turning into last year's battle!" Thomas had to shout to make himself heard.

To their left, they could hear their officers ordering them to wheel about and face the new threat. Once on line, they began to move towards the river. Behind them, the light infantrymen were tumbling back down the hill and forming into a line of their own.

They moved forward together. At the edge of the Little Tennessee, the order to halt was given. Thomas grounded his rifle and watched the regular troops ford the river under the heavy fire of hidden marksmen. Several red-coated bodies drifted downstream. To his right, Sergeant Sanders pointed out hidden positions across the river and called on soldiers armed with rifles to fire on them. A moment later he staggered forward as if he had been punched between the shoulder blades by an invisible hand and dropped to his knees. Before Thomas could react, a flood of bright blood gushed from the sergeant's mouth. He struggled to rise before falling forward onto his face.

"They're behind us!" someone shouted. The crest of the hill was shrouded in smoke as the warriors, who had returned to renew the battle, opened fire. The provincials and light infantry spun about to confront them. Thomas snapped his rifle to his shoulder, took careful aim at a tall warrior dancing along the crest of the hill, and pulled the trigger. The warrior clutched his forehead and took a step backwards before dropping to the ground. Thomas began to reload.

Beside him one of the Rangers, hit squarely in the chest, dropped his musket and stumbled into him. Both men fell to the ground as a swarm of musket balls peppered the area around them. To his right, Thomas heard a low grunt. He turned to see Winslow Driggers, clawing at a wound in his chest, sink to the ground.

"Damn," Winslow hissed through clenched teeth as he dropped his rifle and rolled onto his side. He looked down at the blood oozing between his fingers. He seemed stunned that he could have been hit. He looked towards Thomas and shook his head. "Damn," he repeated. He lowered his head to the ground with a loud sigh.

All about him, Thomas could see men scrambling for cover. They stood behind trees and crouched behind clumps of driftwood and rocks, cursing under their breaths as they reloaded. The metallic *zwing!* of metal ramrods being jerked free of musket barrels sounded all along the line.

"On your feet!" Lieutenant Marion shouted. He jumped up and waved the men forward with a sweeping motion of his sword. "Up and at them!" he cried. "Drive them off."

Inspired by his boldness, Rangers, provincials, and light infantrymen leapt to their feet and surged up the low hillside. Faced with the line of approaching bayonets, the Cherokees abandoned the battle and disappeared over the crest of the hill.

At the top of the hill, the Englishmen dropped to their knees and took long pulls on their canteens. A few men sent desultory shots into the underbrush on the far side as the last of the Cherokees disappeared into it. As quickly as their battle ended, the one on the far bank of the river rumbled back to life. From the top of the hill they could see the regulars were having a hard time of it. Trying to maintain their formations while fighting their way through thick tangles of briars and clumps of driftwood was proving to be almost impossible. Gaps began to appear in their ranks as they fought their way forward. At the base of the hill, a British captain mounted on a white horse appeared. He waved his sword in a circular motion and shouted for the light infantry and provincials to form up and cross the river.

Down the hill they came, heading towards the river at a trot. Half of the men were already fording the river when the Catabwas and white Indians, who had been sent to scout on the far side of the hill, boiled back over the top of it. Within minutes, the beleaguered troops were trudging back up the hotly contested hill and driving the Cherokees before them. Although they had only marched a few miles that morning, many of the men were exhausted by the constant strain of battle. Here and there, men found a tree or rock to hide behind. They sank to the ground to rest as musket and rifle balls zipped overhead.

The see-saw battle continued for two long hours, the Cherokees alternating their attacks from the east, west, and north. At noon, a plea for help from the militia guarding the cattle and pack trains was sent forward. The Cherokees had finally shifted their assault to the almost unprotected rear of the column. The light infantry was ordered to dig in and hold the right flank of the army while Thomas and the other South Carolina troops raced to meet the new attack.

Whipping his mount with the ends of his reins, Thomas urged the animal to greater speed as it plunged into the cane break and raced along the narrow trail to the south. As they broke free of the cane, Thomas felt the horse stumble. The mare regained her footing for a moment before her front legs folded under. Thomas knew instinctively the animal had been hit. He looked down as the animal's head and shoulders hit the ground. He felt himself turning, head over heels, as he was catapulted from the saddle—felt his feet slide free of the stirrups and the reins being snatched from his hands. Ahead of him he saw a large boulder rise from the ground and race to meet him. He had the fleeting impression he was flying.

Loving Lynn Celia

CHAPTER TWENTY-EIGHT

Grant's Battlefield
June 10, 1761

Thomas lay on his back, conscious of the buzzing of hundreds of flies about his face and hands. One of the pesky insects crawled across his cheek and stopped to examine the base of his nose. He brushed it away and opened his eyes. It was night. Overhead, the red glow of a fire danced across the underside of a canvas roof. When he heard the splash of a large fish nearby, he realized he was laying under a fly tent at the edge of the Little Tennessee River. His head ached and his face felt like it was on fire. With a groan, he sat up among his crumpled blankets. A low moan sounded to one side. He turned to find Winslow Driggers on a blanket beside him, his eyes glazed and feverish. Stakes had been driven into the ground behind Winslow's back and across the front of his shoulders to keep him from moving. In his delirium, he kept trying to roll onto his back. He bounced first against the stakes to his rear, then against those in front. An orderly knelt at the wounded man's side and pulled a piece of wet cloth from a canvas bucket. He wrung out the excess water and pulled it across Winslow's forehead.

"Can't you pull up those stakes so's he can get comfortable?" Thomas asked.

The orderly shook his head. "Can't. Poor fellow's shot through the chest and lung. We think the ball's lodged in his shoulder blade. If he don't stay on the wounded side, he'll drown in his own blood." The orderly rose and stepped over Winslow. He bent to inspect the gash on Thomas's forehead. "Dizzy?" he asked.

"A little," Thomas admitted.

"Here." The orderly held out the damp cloth. "Give yourself a good wipe and get some sleep. If you don't have a concussion, you'll be fine tomorrow."

"What if I do?"

"In that case, it'll be about a week."

"I can't stay in the hospital for a week," Thomas croaked. His throat was dry and his lips were cracked and peeling from lack of water. The orderly reached behind Thomas's head and retrieved his canteen. He pulled the cork from the throat and held it out. "It's tepid, but it's wet," he said.

"No thanks," Thomas said. "I'll fill it from the river."

The orderly gave him a dubious look. "I'm a thinkin' you don't want to drink that water," he said. "You see, the colonel don't want his dead dug up and mutilated like Montgomerie's was. So he's ordered they be weighted down and sunk in the river. Must be fifty or sixty corpses in there, not countin' the Indians floating on top." With a nod, Thomas turned up the canteen.

* * * *

Two days later, the army moved north and occupied the abandoned town of Nikwasi. The large council house on the town's mound was converted into a field hospital for the wounded. This town would be spared until last, it would serve as a base for the army while they reduced the middle towns to ashes.

The first evening in Nikwasi, Thomas sat in the grass on the side of the mound, sullen and withdrawn as he looked out over the town. To the south, the flames consuming the small village of Etchoee lit the horizon. Thomas shook his head, trying to imagine what it would be like for Lynn Celia if she had been held in that town. Burned out and chased into hiding twice in one year.

He desperately wanted to return to duty with the Rangers, but each time he mounted a horse, he became so dizzy he almost fell to the ground. The regimental surgeon had convinced him to wait for one week before attempting to go on one of the forays against the nearby Cherokee towns. There would, he said, be plenty of time later. From the information the army had gleaned from the few prisoners it had bothered taking, the valley to the north was full of large and prosperous towns.

It was on the evening of the third day at Nikwasi that Captain Kennedy and Seven Kills climbed the earthen steps of the mound and entered the council house. In one hand the Catabwa carried a piece of bark. He held it out to Thomas. There were letters written in charcoal on its smooth inner side.

"What's it say?" Thomas asked. He handed the bark to the captain.

Kennedy read the words aloud. "It says, Lynn Celia Simpson. 1761. And it's fairly fresh." He held the fragile piece of bark out to Thomas who took it almost reverently. "Where did you find it?" he asked.

"Watauga, a few miles north of here," Kennedy said. "We burned it to the ground this mornin'. It was deserted when we got there except for a few old men and women. We hung the men on the town walls and gave the women to the Catabwas."

Thomas sat and studied the writing long after Captain Kennedy and Seven Kills had departed. He couldn't fight the irresistible urge to run his fingers over the dark marks, thinking to himself as he did so that Lynn Celia had touched this same piece of wood no more than a few days ago. She had left it as a message for him. A message meant to tell him, "I'm alive. There's hope."

From his makeshift bed on the floor of the council house, Winslow encouraged Thomas. He would pause often to cough as he spoke and to wipe away a slow trickle of blood that continued to form at the corner of his mouth. On the third day at Nikwasi, Winslow had propped himself up on one elbow and coughed, then spit the distorted musketball onto the floor of the council house. Since then, he had improved steadily.

"Damnedest thing I ever saw," the doctor said, holding up the ball to inspect it. "Must have been resting inside his lung for it to come out of his mouth like that." He tossed it up and down a few times, catching it in his hand before handing it back to Winslow. "Good thing it was such a small caliber ball. Looks like it came from a pistol. One of the big .75 balls from a Brown Bess would never have come out like that.

You're one lucky devil!"

The orderly, whose name Thomas had learned was VanDalsem, scolded both of them frequently; Winslow for talking and Thomas for listening. "This talkin's gonna be the death of you," he would say to Winslow as he shook his finger in his direction. "Why, I'd bet if you held your nose and blew, the air would shoot straight out of that hole in your back." He would recoil in horror whenever Winslow would tease him by seeming to attempt it.

Martin and Cub came to visit whenever the provincials were in the town, which was often, since they drew the bulk of the garrison duty. Neither of them seemed upset they were missing out on the war. Their adventurous spirit had been satisfied by the two battles on the banks of the Little Tennessee River. They had lain Sergeant Sander's silver inlaid rifle on a blanket alongside Winslow's bed. It had become his prized possession. Still, he had willed it to Thomas, just in case.

Each day brought the news of another town destroyed, but there was little fighting, the spirit of the Cherokees seemed to have been broken.

330

Montgomerie's destruction of their lower towns last year and Grant's burning of the middle towns this one, had taken the fight out of them.

Two weeks after the battle on the Little Tennessee, Thomas was declared fit by the regimental surgeon. He bid a healing Winslow farewell and trooped down the side of the mound to rejoin his company. On the same day, two companies of Highlanders, ragged and weary, returned from the north. They had been sent back to take over the duty of protecting the army's supplies. The provincials, well-rested and bored, marched northward the following morning. They rejoined the army two days later, just in time to aid in the destruction of the last few towns in the valley.

* * * *

Thomas wiped the sweat from his forehead and slung his fingers in a downward arch, spraying the moisture from the tips of his fingers onto the dry ground of the deserted corn field. It hadn't taken long to realize destroying crops and towns was hot and hard work. To the north, the rumble of approaching riders drew his attention to the spot where a column of Captain Kennedy's Catabwas and white Indians moved out of the tree line and headed, single file, towards the small village. There, they counseled with Lieutenant Marion, who shouted to the men in the fields through cupped hands, calling them into the town.

With questioning looks on their faces, they gathered around the officers. It was so still Lieutenant Marion spoke in his normal, quiet tone of voice as he gave them their orders.

"Yesterday evening," he said, "the Catabwas spotted some Cherokees moving along a narrow valley in those mountains over yonder." He poked a finger at a line of misty blue mountains about three miles away. "They don't know they've been spotted." He took a long breath and eyed Thomas. "There are several captives with 'em. Seven Kills thinks one of them is your wife."

A murmur of approval rippled through the loose ranks of provincials. Several of them gave Thomas congratulatory slaps on his shoulders and back.

Lieutenant Marion grinned and nodded his head. "There aren't any warriors with them, so we're going to ride ahead and set up an ambush at the far end of the valley." The inflection in his voice changed. "Do not shoot!" he cautioned the men. "If we can surround them before they're able to scatter, they're apt to surrender. They've been beat

down and most of the fight has gone out of them."
His head spun around to Martin who stood to one
side, his arms folded and his hips resting against a
stack of hand-hewn lumber. "I understand they
have elected you as their sergeant," the lieutenant
said. "Choose ten men and follow Captain
Kennedy. You'll be under his command until you
return. Any questions?"

When no one spoke up, he dismissed the men
who saddled their mounts and followed Captain
Kennedy to the north.

* * * *

Thomas checked the priming in the pan of his
musket for the third time. He had left his rifle in its
scabbard when he had surrendered the reins of his
mount to one of the men selected to stay with the
horses. If this happened to turn into a fight, it
would be a close-in fight. There would be no need
for long-range accuracy. He reached out and tested
the point of his bayonet with the index finger of his
left hand, checked the priming once again, and
rested his back against the large boulder behind
him. Down below, he could make out the narrow
footpath that wound its way along a small, clear-
flowing stream. The water lapped and gurgled as it

meandered around the roots and rocks that littered the streambed. Off to his left, a sudden flash of color caught his attention. He could see Martin and Seven Kills lean forward in anticipation as the shuffling sounds of feet moving through dry leaves increased. His heart leapt into his throat when he thought he spied Lynn Celia. Even without seeing her face, he identified her by the part in her dark hair and, with her smooth walk, he told himself he would have been able to spot her a mile away.

The party consisted of thirty women and about twice as many children. A single, gray-haired warrior led the way, his head moving from side to side as he stepped along. He came to a halt almost directly below Thomas and threw up his hand, seeming to sense something was wrong. Turning to face the line of women and children, he motioned for them to move off the trail and take cover. He cocked his musket and began to move ahead slowly and cautiously. Before the warrior had advanced more than a few steps, the padding sounds of moccasined feet could be heard coming up the trail from the rear of the column. Within a few moments, three more warriors had joined him at the front of the line. Two carried captured Brown Bess muskets, the third tapped the blunt side of a shiny French-made tomahawk against the outside of one thigh. All four men seemed to know they had been caught. The one with the tomahawk stood in the center of the trail, his mouth open as he turned in a slow circle and looked up at the steep hillside. He spoke to the other men. The words were foreign to Thomas, but he caught their meaning as clearly as if the man had spoken in English.

Slowly, the men began to back away. One of them held his right hand against his leg and surreptitiously motioned for the women and children to back away. The hillside came alive with the unmistakable sounds of muskets being drawn to full cock. It was obvious to the Cherokees down below they were facing at least a hundred men. One of them lowered the stock of his musket to the ground. He looked up the hillside again and called, "Kennedy!" It was not a question; they knew who had tracked them down.

The Captain called to them in their language, telling them to lay their weapons on the ground and send their captives forward. The younger warrior with the tomahawk snapped a few angry words at the older man, urging him to fight. The other warriors shook their heads and dropped their weapons. Captain Kennedy stepped from behind a large tree and leveled his musket at the young warrior's chest. He didn't say a word, he didn't need to. The warrior made a sound of disgust and flung the tomahawk into the bushes. He folded his arms and scowled up at his captor. The older warrior glowered at the young man and barked an order in the direction of the women and children. Three women moved out of the bushes and into the center of the trail. Thomas eyed them. Each of the women had a different shade of hair: blonde, red, or black. An involuntary groan escaped Thomas when he realized the dark-haired woman wasn't Lynn Celia. Overcome by disappointment, he sank to one knee, watching half-heartedly as Captain Kennedy's men slid down the steep hillside and began to herd the prisoners together into a single compact group.

The Captain spoke at length with the older warrior who would answer in short, choppy sentences, sometimes gesturing with his hand in one direction, sometimes in another. When the captain was satisfied he had learned everything the man knew, he pointed to Thomas and motioned for him to come down onto the trail. Thomas slid down the slope, using branches of mountain laurel to slow his descent. Once on the trail he paused long enough to dust off the seat of his breeches before throwing a half-hearted salute to the officer. "Sir?"

The captain indicated the warrior with a jerk of his thumb. "He says there were two more captives, a man and a woman. They slipped off last night. He's certain they headed south, but nobody bothered to look for them. They're all too eager to get away from the army." He paused to study Thomas's face for a moment. "I'm sorry, that's all he knows. He wasn't from the village she was held in."

"Doesn't anyone know the woman's name?" Thomas asked. His voice was heavy with disappointment.

Kennedy shook his head. "He doesn't know." Turning away, he motioned to his men. "Head 'em back over the trail we came by," he called to the men. "We'll turn them over to the regulars when we get back to Nikwasi."

* * * *

That evening, Thomas sat alongside Martin, poking at the coals of their cooking fire as they waited for a pot of salt pork and water to come to a boil. The ten men still remaining in Thomas's company had been left behind in the small village of Kanuga when the regulars had marched away

337

that afternoon as an escort for a long line of forlorn and sullen Cherokee prisoners.

Martin looked up as Cub stepped into the circle of firelight. Cub held the front of his hunting shirt folded up with one hand. Inside, were a dozen small potatoes and a few carrots. "I found these in one of the food bins over by the council house," he said to Martin. "I washed the dirt off 'em down at the river." He pushed the bottom of his frock over the copper pot and let the carrots and potatoes slide into the water. "That ought to fill us up," he said, flapping the hem of the garment to dislodge a few stray drops of water. He dropped down alongside Thomas and pulled a small leather bag from the inside of his shirt. He fished around inside the bag with his fingers and removed a short-stemmed pipe. "Anybody got some tobacco left?" he asked, looking around at the circle of faces gathered about the fire. One of the men tossed a pouch to him across the fire.

"Obliged," Cub said. He tamped a pinch of tobacco into the bowl of the pipe. "The lieutenant says we're to fire the town tomorrow and march back down the valley to Nikwasi." He paused long enough to light the pipe with a twig from the fire. "Looks like we'll be heading back to Fort Prince George." He took a long pull on the pipe, held the smoke in for a moment to savor its taste, and blew a long gray stream upward into the night air. "The lieutenant says the Cherokees are about done in. He expects them to ask for terms any day."

Grunts of approval sounded about the fire. "The sooner the better," one of the men chimed in. He stuck his hand inside his coat and thrust it out through a rip in the material. "Between the holes in my jacket and those in my pants, it gets a might airy at night." A rumble of low laughter erupted from the other soldiers whose clothes were as ragged as those of the speaker.

One of the sentries, guarding the open gates of the town's wall, hissed a warning to the men at the fire. They sprang to their feet and grabbed their weapons. They were all nervous and acutely aware of how few they were if a war party of Cherokees showed up.

"What is it?" Martin asked as the men slipped into defensive positions along the wall of the town. The sentry pointed towards the dark treeline on the far side of the open field. "Someone's movin' out there," he answered in a low voice.

Thomas checked his priming and thrust the muzzle of his musket between the upright posts. Behind him, one of the men threw a deer hide over the fire, leaving the anxious men in darkness. As his eyes grew accustomed to the night, Thomas could make out movement inside the distant forest. Two figures emerged from the darkened treeline. They halted at the outside edge of the cornfield and shifted about uncertainly. The outlines were clearly those of a man and a woman.

"No one fire, unless I do!" Martin hissed over his shoulder.

The figures started, startled. The muted sound of Martin's warning had carried across the open space to them. After a moment of hesitation the man began to step backwards, in the direction of the forest. The woman wavered for a moment, unsure of the danger, before following him.

"Should I hail to 'em, or kill 'em?" Martin asked Lieutenant Marion who had moved up to stand at his elbow. "If they make it back into those woods, we won't be able to follow them 'til tomorrow."

Martin thrust his face in the direction of the distant figures in an attempt to see more clearly. "Less I miss my guess, the man's wearin' a loincloth," he said. "And the woman's hair is in braids."

The lieutenant hesitated. He looked from Thomas to Martin. Both men were all but invisible in the meager light shed by the narrow sliver of moon overhead.

"Sergeant, you take a bead on that man out there," he whispered to keep his voice from carrying. "Simpson, grab that rifle of yours and aim at the woman. If they turn to run when I call out, shoot 'em."

Thomas steadied his rifle against one of the uprights of the town wall. He fingered the trigger as he struggled to place the bead of the front sight on the far target. In the darkness, it was all but impossible to align both sights. "I can't get a bead on her," he said to the lieutenant without taking the weapon from his shoulder

"I feared as much," Marion replied. "It'll be a miracle if either of you hit your mark in this darkness." He cast a quick glance from left to right and leaned forward like a runner preparing for a race. "Get ready."

He called out, "Put your hands up!" His voice startled a pair of deer bedded down in the middle of the field. The two animals jumped to their feet and scrambled towards the woods. They both veered sharply when they sensed the two figures at the edge of the field. Thomas lowered his weapon and blew a relieved breath; he had come within a hair's breadth of pulling the trigger.

The lieutenant called to the two figures again. After a moment's hesitation, there was a sudden yelp of elation as the two figures realized they were hearing English.

"You're Englishmen!" The man shouted across the field.

"That we are," Marion called back.

With a whoop, the man reached out and took the woman's arm, escorting her towards the town at a fast walk.

"We weren't sure if the Cherokees were still here," the man explained as soon as he came through the gate. "Thank the Lord you called out when you did. At first, we couldn't tell if you were speakin' English or Cherokee. We were just about to make a run for it." The man thrust his hand in the lieutenant's direction. "Name's David Foster," he said with a grin.

"Please to make your acquaintance, sir. You're safe now," Lieutenant Marion assured him. Tipping his hat, he tilted his head respectfully in the woman's direction. "Mrs. Foster?"

"No," the woman said in a raspy voice. "My name's Simpson, Lynn Celia Simpson. I was taken at Ninety-Six a year ago."

Thomas's heart leapt into his throat. In the darkness, with her hair in two tight braids, he hadn't even recognized her! When he thought of having taken aim at her, of how close he had been to pulling the trigger! He doubled over and threw up.

One of the men jerked the deer hide off of the fire and threw a handful of dry grass onto the coals. Within seconds it flared back to life, illuminating the interior of the small Cherokee town.

Thomas called Lynn Celia's name and staggered towards his wife. Lynn Celia threw herself into his arms. They both burst into tears. The men averted their eyes and drifted away, acting as if the two weeping people did not exist.

Loving Lynn Celia

G.G. Stokes, Jr.

EPILOGUE

Lynn Celia's life fluttered away one minute after the big clock on her mantle chimed twelve midnight, signaling her one-hundredth birthday. The clock had been a gift to her from Thomas on their twenty-sixth wedding anniversary. He had traded off the rifle he had carried through two wars to get it. He remembered her scolding him for his rashness. That had been fifty years ago.

Thomas reached out and gathered her into his arms as her breathing, which had grown labored during the night, grew more erratic and faint. At the end, with a sigh, it ceased. He burst into tears. He had never felt so alone in his life.

The following day, at noon, when their large brood of children and grandchildren, and great-grandchildren and great-great-grandchildren, pulled the latch string and stepped into the darkened cabin bearing birthday gifts, they found them lying side by side on the bed Thomas had fashioned with his own hands. Their faces were peaceful and content.

Loving Lynn Celia

Thomas Simpson had spent his life loving Lynn Celia. He could not have imagined a world without her.

The End

Please take a few moments to rate this book. Thank you!

G.G. Stokes, Jr.

ALSO BY G.G. STOKES, JR.

The Colonial Southeast Series

The Road to Bloody Marsh
A Lesser Form of Patriotism
Letters for Catherine

Mystery/Crime

Fireson Bay
Fireson Bay: Resurrection
Fireson Bay: Pink Roses

Nonfiction

Massacre at Roanoke
Camp Toccoa: First Home of the Airborne